A Simple Twist of Fate

A Novel by Marianne Evans

Based on the Motion Picture from Touchstone Pictures

Executive Producer Steve Martin

Based on the Screenplay Written by Steve Martin

Produced by Ric Kidney

Directed by Gillies MacKinnon

A SIGNET BOOK

SIGNET

Published by the Penguin Group
Penguin Books Ltd, 27 Wrights Lane, London W8 5TZ, England
Penguin Books USA Inc., 375 Hudson Street, New York, New York 10014, USA
Penguin Books Australia Ltd, Ringwood, Victoria, Australia
Penguin Books Canada Ltd, 10 Alcorn Avenue, Toronto, Ontario, Canada M4V 3B2
Penguin Books (NZ) Ltd, 182–190 Wairau Road, Auckland 10, New Zealand

Penguin Books Ltd, Registered Offices: Harmondsworth, Middlesex, England

First published in the USA by Signet, an imprint of Dutton Signet, 1994
Published in Signet 1995
1 3 5 7 9 10 8 6 4 2

Printed in England by Clays Ltd, St Ives plc

TRIAL TIME

Things didn't look good for Michael McCann in his court fight to keep Mathilda as his daughter.

The man he was fighting, John Newland, was as popular and rich as he was shrewd and handsome—and Newland had the judge in his back pocket.

The woman who was Michael's only character witness, April Simon, was considered only slightly less kooky than Michael.

Even little Mathilda had been wooed with the gift of a horse and the promise of a privileged life.

All Michael had on his side was heart—and his heart had been shattered once before. Now it seemed primed to crack wide open once again. . . .

Prologue

Michael McCann never saw it coming. One moment he was a happily married man, employed in a job he loved; in the next, his life was in ruins.

The events of that seemingly ordinary Monday were burned into his memory, and in the unhappy years that followed, Michael lived that day over and over again.

Michael was a school teacher and Mondays began with fifth grade homeroom, then progressed in normal fashion through fourth grade American history, recess, study hall, and on into midmorning chorus with the sixth grade. The only incident out of the ordinary that day was a phone call from his wife, Elaine.

Choir practice, which Michael conducted three times a week, allowed him to combine the best part of his job: kids and chorus. The whole school echoed with the sounds of Michael's class singing its collective heart out while the chorus accompanist, Mrs. Crebbs, banged out the music on a battered upright piano. Michael stood conducting in front of the two rows of children, a smile on his face. But he found it hard to concentrate on the music that morning. His mind kept returning to his brief conversation with Elaine.

"The results of the amnio are in," Elaine said matter-of-factly. "I need to see you."

Elaine was six months pregnant, a pregnancy that had so far been routine—not that Michael ever stopped worrying about his wife's health or that of their unborn child. And this was the moment that filled every prospective parent with dread—amniocentesis, the test that Elaine had taken the week before, foretold the well-being and the sex of the child. Amnio could also foretell birth defects that would change the life of the baby and its parents forever.

For a moment, Michael couldn't breathe. His throat constricted, his voice choked, and his words became disjointed as a dozen thoughts pulsed through his brain. "I . . . Is . . . Are you?"

"The baby is fine, Michael," said Elaine reassuringly. "Absolutely fine. Trust me."

The coil of fear that had cinched tight in Michael's chest loosened a little. Coherent speech would take longer to return, but he could already feel relief like a soothing warmth in his veins.

"I'll be over in about an hour," said Elaine. She had hung up without saying more.

Michael was mystified. He closed his eyes and tried to recall her few words, struggling to hear her voice again, as if replaying a tape in his mind. She had sounded tired, he decided, her voice a little strained, a bit wrung out. Of course, it was natural—she had been just as anxious about the test results as he had been. It was only normal that such intense emotions should show up in her voice.

Then why was she so anxious to see him?

Suddenly, the answer shot into his mind. The sex! The sex of the baby was determined by amniocentesis. Michael and Elaine had agreed that they didn't want to be told in advance, but now it was suddenly quite obvious that the doctor had let the secret out. Elaine was on her way, bursting to tell him if they were going to have a little boy or a little girl.

Michael chuckled to himself, ruefully shaking his head at his ridiculous propensity for imagining the worst when the best was close at hand. *Now* he heard his wife's voice clearly: "The *baby* is fine, Michael, absolutely fine. . . Trust me."

So, all through choir practice the same thoughts had been buzzing through his brain. Boy? Or girl? A boy would be nice—better than nice. A boy would be *great*! The things you can do with a boy: baseball games, fishing, camping trips . . .

But then he thought: Why couldn't a little girl do the same things? You could play baseball with a girl, you could take her camping, fishing. . . . Not that Michael had ever been much of a camper or fisherman, but, like a lot of first-time parents, he assumed that somehow these skills were issued to you when you got the baby.

Michael's mind went around and around on the question until he was sure of only one thing: He didn't *care* what sex his child was. Boy, girl—it didn't matter. All he wanted was a *baby*; happy and healthy and he would be content.

As his sixth grade choir sang, Michael examined the children, looking from face to face. That girl was a better singer than most; that one was a math whiz. That girl couldn't seem to get the hang of elementary French; that boy was a klutz on the playing field. They were all different, these children, with their own strengths and weaknesses. Simultaneously they were genetic reflections of their parents and unique individuals, original in themselves.

Michael could only hope that his unborn son—or daughter—took the best of his character and left his weaknesses. The one talent Michael did possess, he hoped to pass along to his child, son or daughter. He was a skilled carpenter, a woodworker so adept at making fine furniture that he could, he suspected, make a living at it if he ever decided to give up teaching. Not that he ever would . . .

Michael was so lost in his reverie that it took him a moment or two to realize that a fellow teacher, Tommy Black, had leaned into the chorus room.

"Michael," he stage-whispered, "could I see you for a minute?"

Michael nodded, assuming that Elaine had arrived, and turned to the accompanist. "Mrs. Crebbs, would you take over? I won't be long."

Mrs. Crebbs's eyes never left her sheet music as her fingers continued to pound the keys. "Okay, Mr. McCann."

Michael stole into the corridor, fully expecting to see his wife waiting for him. Instead, Tommy took his arm and walked him a few feet down the hallway.

"She's not here yet?" asked Michael nervously.

"Not yet," said Tommy. "Calm down."

"Calm?" Michael smiled. "How can I be calm when I'm about to find out—"

"What are you hoping for?" asked Tommy quickly. "A boy or a girl?"

"I don't care," said Michael, trying to sound like he meant it. "*And* I don't want to know. I'm old-fashioned that way, you know?"

Tommy nodded as if he understood perfectly, but he looked puzzled. "If you don't want to know, then how come she's coming over here to tell you?"

It was all Michael could do to try to contain his excitement. "I don't *want* to know, but I'm *dying* to know."

Tommy smiled and dug something out of his trouser pocket. "Look, this is for the kid." He held out his palm. Lying in his hand was an American Eagle gold piece, shimmering in the strong morning sunlight.

"It's a little early for baby presents, isn't it?" Michael was taken aback. Then his curiosity got the better of him and he peered closely at the coin.

"It's one ounce of solid gold," said Tommy. His voice was hushed, almost reverent.

"The baby isn't born yet," said Michael, "and you want him to go into banking."

Tommy shook his head. "No . . . That's not it. But it *is* money in the bank. By the time the kid gets to be twenty-one, it'll be worth so much it'll pay for a new car, maybe even finance a college education. One thing for sure—it's always there for you when you need it." He placed the coin in Michael's hand.

Michael hefted it in his palm, balancing it like an assayer. He had never realized how much a single ounce could weigh.

"Who can say how much it will be worth?" mused Tommy.

At the far end of the corridor, a door was swung open and Elaine walked in. She was too faraway for Michael to make out her face, but he could see that she held a sheaf of papers. He swallowed hard and winked at Black.

"Well, here we go," he said as he started down the hallway toward his wife.

All his life, Michael McCann had masked nervousness with humor, wisecracking his way through any situation that made him jittery and tense.

"Well, well, well," he said, dancing down the hall. "What's it going to be? A little Matthew?" He stopped and his eyes grew wide as if actually gazing upon a newborn boy named Matthew. "Great name! Gotta admit it, right? A great name. He'll be . . ." Michael searched the air around his head, like a wine connoisseur looking for exactly the right term to describe a rare vintage.

"Cowardly and nervous," he said finally. "Cowardly and nervous, just like his dad." Michael continued to gambol toward Elaine. "You know . . . I'd love him to be president. Not of the United States, of course—but Microsoft! I'll give him my old computer to teethe on. . . . But wait!"

Michael stopped, frozen in his tracks as if a thunderbolt of a thought had struck. "But wait! What if it's a girl?" Michael's mouth dropped open as if such a notion had never, ever, in his wildest dreams, occurred to him. "A name! We need a name!" His brow wrinkled as he thought about it for a moment.

Then his eyes lit up. "Mathilda! Yes, Mathilda! Sweet Mathilda of the Lowlands. I know it's your mother's name, but have you considered changing mothers? Maybe you could change to a Kathy, or perhaps, a Susan."

He was close enough to Elaine now to see the expression on her face. She hadn't responded at all to his humor. In fact, she looked bleak and drained, as if exhausted by her own emotions. Instantly, his mood changed.

"What? What is it?" he said quickly. "What's the matter? Are you all right?"

Elaine nodded wearily. "Yes."

"Is the baby all right?" For a moment, Michael did not want to hear the answer.

Elaine nodded again. "The baby is all right, Michael. . . . It's this." She held up the medical report.

"What is it?" he demanded, snatching the papers from her hand. He studied them for a moment, but the words printed on the institutional gray paper refused to make sense to his eyes.

"Elaine," he said quietly. "What is going on? What is this thing?"

Elaine sighed heavily. "It's a test I had done. Something that isn't normally part of the amnio."

"What kind of test?"

"A genetic test, Michael."

There was a long tortured pause as Michael strove to make sense of this piece of information. "A genetic test? What do we need that for?"

"I had a reason," said Elaine. "It's not yours, Michael. *She's* not yours." Her eyes left her husband's face, looking over his shoulder to Tommy who stood still at the far end of the corridor. Michael turned to follow the line of her gaze, catching a glimpse of Tommy as he darted into an empty classroom.

Michael felt a cold, paralyzing fear creep over him. His knees felt rubbery. Something heavy and constricting shifted in his chest as he tried to understand the few simple, crippling words his wife had uttered.

"How could you do this?" he whispered. "How could you do this to someone who loved you?"

It was a question she had asked herself a million times before, yet she had no answer. Seeing her husband standing before her, broken by the pain of her betrayal, she felt as if a piece of her soul had shattered. At that momemt she hated herself and hated what she had done to a man she had once loved so much.

Elaine McCann had tears in her eyes. "We're not all perfect like you, Michael."

1

Five Years Later

Michael McCann had changed. He was tougher, withdrawn, defeated, and his old good humor had been replaced with a dour, gloomy air—but the pain of Elaine's betrayal had remained constant.

The biggest changes in the sad life of Michael McCann had been a change of address and a change of profession. Burrows, Virginia, pop. 12,000, in the Blue Ridge mountains of Virginia, was the sort of picture-book town where neighbors knew their neighbors and front doors were left unlocked. It was a happy town, and if Michael McCann wasn't happy exactly, at least he had a pretty place in which he could be profoundly miserable. In a funny kind of way, he fit right in—not because he was so disconsolate, but because he was a welcome addition to Burrows's already considerable collection of eccentrics. He was the object of great interest to the loungers and time killers on Main Street, who caught glimpses of him on his rare visits to town. To the children of Burrows, this morose, taciturn outsider was, of course, nothing less than the bogey man come to life in their midst.

The other change in Michael McCann's life was the way he made his living. When his world collapsed, it collapsed completely. He couldn't continue at his old job. Working side by side with Tommy Black would have been an impossibly painful situation, and he found when he landed a job at another school that his heart just wasn't in it anymore. After a few despondent months of teaching, Michael walked away from his career and settled in Burrows. It was there that he took up the tools to make his living at a skill he never thought he would need—carpentry.

Working with wood became his single-minded passion. Michael toiled endlessly at making furniture, working all day and often deep into the night as well. Every piece had to be perfect. A flaw in the wood or a fault in his own craftsmanship was enough to make him scrap the entire piece. Michael was not too good on the sales end of his one-man business, but his reputation for excellence ensured a constant stream of commissions.

He worked, he slept, and he rarely emerged from his dark, little house on the edge of town. And that was the bitter, barren life of Michael McCann.

If Michael McCann stood at one end of the human spectrum in Burrows, Virginia, then John Newland was faraway at the other end of the scale.

Newland, a slim and handsome man in his early thirties, carried himself with the ease and authority of one born with great charm and great wealth. He was a Hunt Country patrician, the scion of an old Virginia family that traced its roots back to before the foundation of the Republic and that sent more than a dozen Newlands to Virginia's House of Burgesses throughout two centuries.

John Newland was just the latest in a long lineage of rich, patriotic men who had never, it seemed, put a foot wrong on the path of history.

Of course, this sort of monotonous, multigenerational success did not happen by accident. For generations, for hundreds of years, the Newlands had been known as shrewd dealers, tough negotiators, and astute businessmen—politics being only one of the family enterprises. The portraits of the Newland ancestors which hung in the elegant rooms of the family estate showed men and women with hard, rather austere faces, knowing eyes and hard mouths—features which suggested that the family had known how to play the power game since time immemorial.

That John Newland and Michael McCann should meet one cool autumn morning was not all that odd; they were playing out the parts that life and class had cast for them. John Newland had ordered an oak refectory table from Michael, and he had come to deliver it. Michael was trundling his handiwork up to the estate, and encountered John Newland, wearing a polo shirt and jodhpurs, black knee boots and riding gloves.

Newland was passing through as Michael and Newland's estate manager, Tom, hefted the heavy piece into place. The new owner nodded appreciatively.

"Nice work," Newland said, heading out of the room. At the door he called over his shoulder, "Tom, cut a check for Mr. McCann."

"Yes, sir."

Michael stood awkwardly in the middle of the room, his eyes down, stealing glances at his table. Tom wrote a check quickly and handed it to the carpenter, but Michael seemed to be rooted to the spot.

"Is there anything else?" Tom asked.

"Feel the top."

Tom rubbed his hand across the smooth and perfectly finished wood. "Very nice."

"Yep," said Michael with a sigh. He walked slowly, reluctantly toward the door as if unwilling to leave his creation, like a parent forced to leave his beloved child among strangers.

Burrows was in the heart of hunt country and horses were a way of life for the upper classes of the town and the surrounding countryside. One of the high points of the equine social season was the Burrows Hunt Club charity polo match. It was a casual competition, quite unlike the serious play during the regular season, and it always drew a large crowd.

All of the Burrows's horse set turned out for the event, including the Lammeter sisters, Daisy and Nancy, the daughters of Jason Lammeter.

The Lammeters were Burrows's second most prominent family after the Newlands.

Both of the Lammeter women were pretty, blue-eyed, ash blondes in their early twenties. Both were blessed with sharp senses of humor. And it was there that all resemblance ended.

Nancy wore her hair long and soft; Daisy, in her perennial state of rebellion, had her hair cropped short. Nancy dressed in the manner of her age and social station: tweeds, skirts, Hermés scarfs, a sort of preppy-chic-meets-Lands-End; Daisy favored bright colors or funereal black, wildly decorated or state penitentiary severe.

Daisy liked to drink, smoke, and shoot pool in less than savory establishments; Nancy took wine with dinner and, perhaps, a little champagne on special occasions. Nancy was serious and studious and in her last year of law school at the University of Virginia; Daisy had barely scraped through high school and had dropped out of Tidewater Community College after a single, tortured inglorious semester.

But both had looked forward to the polo match. For Nancy it was a beautiful day to be in the open air, to see old friends and to enjoy the game. Daisy wanted to go because she liked to watch men in tight pants. Despite their differences, the sisters were the best of friends.

As Daisy said: "It's a perfect partnership. Nancy is a lawyer and *I'm* a lawbreaker."

All eyes were on John Newland as he pulled up to the edge of the polo field in his black Mercedes.

Most liked what they saw; a few did not. In the stands, not far from Nancy and Daisy was Newland's brother, Tanny, a thin, sallow-faced young man. Tanny's head was always filled with schemes to get rich—and to get independent—quick, as well as a collection of harebrained ideas and well-nourished grudges. He had a terrible temper, a disposition made more volatile when mixed with alcohol (a substance of which Tanny was inordinately fond), and his resentment and envy of his brother knew no bounds.

Tanny Newland longed to tell Big Brother and the narrow little world of Burrows, Virginia, just what they could do. He wanted nothing more than to kick over the traces and get out of town for good, to make his way in the wider world—except there was one small problem: he had no capital and he hated work of any shape or form. Tanny's only income was a small amount of interest paid to him every month, dividends earned on his inheritance which was held in trust. Until he was old enough to get his hands on the full sum—or unless he hit the Virginia lottery—he was tied to John Newland and forced to rage against his brother's success and endure his brother's thinly veiled contempt. Tanny Newland was not completely without power in his own family, though. He knew where a body or two happened to be buried and one day, when the time was right (or the next time he was in deep, deep trouble) he might be forced to dig them up. . . .

John Newland had his supporters and detractors even on his own polo team. Randy Keating, a well-established lawyer in Burrows and a member of a Virginia family just as old as John Newland's own, liked and admired him. His teammate Jerry Bryce took a dimmer view. The two men were putting their polo ponies through their paces when Newland arrived at the field, but they slowed their mounts to a trot to watch the golden boy of Burrows make his entrance.

Newland had taken a polished polo saddle from the trunk of his Mercedes, and was ambling toward them, the saddle slung nonchalantly over his arm.

"Here comes your hero," said Bryce acidly.

Keating smiled. "Why do I have the feeling you're not going to vote for him?"

Bryce may not have liked John Newland, but he knew there was no point in being obviously unpleasant to a man who was on the verge of launching a promising political career. He creased a smile onto his lips and did his best to look friendly, telling himself that there would come a day when he would cross swords with John Newland. Until that day came, he could wait.

"How's it going, John?" said Bryce, feeling like a phony.

"Not bad Bryce, not bad . . ." Then John Newland looked puzzled, staring at the empty saddle on his arm. "Oh, shit! I forgot the horse."

Keating laughed extravagantly, while Bryce managed a grin, even though he thought the joke rather lame.

* * *

Despite its genteel pretensions, polo was a fast-paced, take-no-prisoners game—roughly equivalent to a game of NHL hockey played on horseback instead of ice—even a friendly match like this charity event. The four players on each team had to cover an immense field, racing from one end to the other, from goal to goal, in a matter of seconds. The ball, while weighing only a few ounces, flew through the air with the velocity of a bullet and could do real injury if it happened to strike flesh and bone. Bruising collisions between riders were common, the mounts slamming into each other as the horsemen battled for the ball.

Good horsemanship, the ability to handle a mallet and a hefty dose of daring made for a distinguished polo player and John Newland was a master of the game. He was not above a little show boating either. Early in the first of six, seven-minute periods John Newland rammed home a goal, swinging his mallet powerfully, the ball whistling by Bryce's head and into the net.

Newland pulled hard on the reins and his horse wheeled and galloped back toward the center of the field. There was a burst of applause from the spectators and he raised a gloved hand in acknowledgment.

"There's a fine goal from John Newland," the match announcer trumpeted. This was Cal Mosely, the editor of the local newspaper and an unabashed Newland supporter. "A goal from the man who is soon to be our representative in

Washington—that is, if his money means anything at all. . . .''

There was laughter from the crowd and some scattered clapping. John Newland knew how to take a little good-natured ribbing. He brought his horse to a halt directly in front of the announcer's table.

''Tell them to vote for me, Cal,'' he shouted. ''Not only do I promise world peace, I'll also fix those potholes on Stewart Street.''

There was more laughter from the crowd as Newland trotted back onto the field as the polo match resumed. The instant the ball was back in play, John Newland spurred his horse into a gallop and swung his mallet, clipping the ball away from Bryce and driving it down the line of riders. Bryce charged after it, but Keating got between him and the ball, slamming into the rider like a football blocker—an illegal move, but worth it, Keating figured, to let Newland look good.

Tanny Newland lounged in the stands, between two pretty girls, a dismissive sneer on his pale face. It was typical of his brother to be able to show off so shamelessly, campaign for votes like a ward heeler, steal the ball from a teammate, and still have people love him.

''Your brother is so great!'' exclaimed one of the girls. ''Really great.''

Tanny Newland smiled stiffly. ''Yeah, he's *really* great. We're so proud, ya know?''

A few moments later Tanny was pleased to see that, for once, someone got the better of his brother. John Newland was driving up the field, his mallet thrashing like a whip, bearing down on the ball, seconds away, it seemed, from scoring another goal. But out of nowhere came Bryce, pouncing on the ball, smashing it out from under John Newland's mallet, through the legs of the horse and deftly bringing it under his control.

"That's Jerry Bryce," Cal announced. "As a lawyer, he's up and coming, or is it down and going . . . ?"

John Newland didn't have time to enjoy the joke. He was too busy trying to control his horse, his mount having been thrown into confusion by Jerry Bryce's skillful play. He stood up in his stirrups and pulled back on his reins, bringing his horse to a halt just a few feet from the stands. Instantly, his eyes settled on Daisy and Nancy Lammeter. The game forgotten, he engaged Nancy and flashed her his most charming smile. Nancy, for her part, was unbending, seemingly immune to his charm, and did not return his knowing grin.

She had known John Newland for most of her life, in all the different ports of call for someone growing up in Burrows—in high school, in dancing class, at the junior cotillion. She had never liked him—of course, no one could like him as much as he *loved* himself.

John Newland knew her too, but he insisted on an elaborate pantomime of thinking for a moment, as if searching his mind for some small, arcane piece of information. Finally, he came up with it.

"Nancy Lammeter," he said.

"Nice to meet you, Nancy," Nancy shot back.

John Newland laughed and then spurred his horse back into the fast and furious action on the field. From then on, every time Newland made a flashy move—and he made many—he glanced over toward Nancy, as if dedicating every maneuver to her. Where many of the women in the grandstand would have been flattered by such attention, such public flirting made Nancy feel slightly uncomfortable. She nudged Daisy in the ribs.

"Let's get some lunch," she said.

"Sure, but nothing elaborate. I have to get to the store. I'm a working girl, remember?" Daisy didn't really care all that much about her job and would have blown it off if she found something better to do. But the polo match, men in tight pants and all, hadn't interested her much and besides, no one was paying any attention to *her*.

But she was wrong. Tanny had noticed her. Nancy Lammeter was just right for his brother; Daisy was much more Tanny's cup of tea. He liked girls who were a little on the wild side and that certainly was Daisy's reputation around town. He decided that sometime in the near future he was going to have to get to know her.

But Tanny didn't quite have the panache of his brother when it came to making an impression on the ladies. As the sisters drove off the field in Nancy's bright red Honda, John Newland left the game once again, raced along behind the car, and gallantly tipped his helmet to her.

"Oh brother," said Nancy.

"Must be nice to have admirers like that," Daisy observed archly.

"Please . . ." said Nancy.

"Hey, enjoy it."

As the car disappeared down the road, Newland tore back into the game, effortlessly threading himself back into the action. He snagged the ball and fired a shot on goal, the ball slamming into the net. There were more cheers and applause from all the onlookers—except, of course, from Tanny Newland, who felt that ever familiar sense of resentment boiling inside of him.

2

Every so often, the regulars at the Rainbow Bar on Burrows's main street were treated to one of the stranger sights their little town had to offer. It was a simple scene, one which in another, less nosy town no one would ever notice: Michael McCann, head down, stumping along the street to his usual destination, a junk shop going by the whimsical name of "Mrs. Simon's Coins, Antiques and Hoo-Ha."

Joe, the bartender, manager, and resident philosopher of the Rainbow spotted Michael first. He gestured toward the window with his chin.

"There he goes, every week, regular as clockwork."

The only other patron in the tavern, a burly quarry worker called Rob took a sip of his beer. " 'Course, it's none of our business what he's doing." Nevertheless, he slipped off his barstool and peered out the window. "Where is he?"

"There," said Joe, pointing down the block.

Rob caught sight of Michael just as he vanished inside the ramshackle, shingled building that stood just in from the street, its dusty windows perpetually obscured with rusty security gates. It wasn't that the proprietor, Mrs. Simon, worried all that much about security—burglary was extremely uncommon in Burrows—it was more that she couldn't be bothered taking the bars down every morning only to put them back every evening. The store was a cross between a pawn shop and a real antiques' store. There were some things worth stealing in Mrs. Simon's shop, but there was a lot of worthless junk, too—rooms of it—and it would take a skilled thief to hunt out the few kernels of valuable wheat among a lot of shabby chaff.

Rob watched the door of the shop swing shut, but kept his eyes on it just in case something exciting happened.

"Must be payday," he said.

"Leave the poor guy alone."

With some difficulty, Rob tore his eyes from the empty street and turned back to his beer. "I met this schoolteacher guy," he said. "And he knew McCann 'bout five, six years ago. Said he actually had a personality once upon a time. He musta hocked it in Mrs. Simon's store, 'cause he sure ain't got one now."

"Yeah . . . well . . ." Joe put a glass under one of the beer taps and filled it to the brim. "He's not bothering anybody, so why not just leave him be." With a skilled and practiced motion he slid the beer glass down the bar where it came to stop in front of an empty stool.

Rob looked puzzled. "Who's that for?"

"Him," said Joe. "Hey, Tanny. How you doin'? How'd the game go?"

Tanny Newland pushed through the double doors of the Rainbow and settled before the tall, cool beer. "Good," he said, reaching for his glass.

"How'd your brother do?" the bartender asked.

Tanny wiped the beer foam from his upper lip. "Okay, I guess," he said with a shrug. "He fumbled a bit."

"Again, huh? Must be slipping." There was the slightest edge of sarcasm in Joe's voice.

Tanny's disaffection with his brother was no big secret around the Rainbow Bar. When Tanny got a couple of beers in him, he tended to run his mouth on the subject of the golden boy in the Newland family. Career bartenders like Joe knew that few people were more likely to tell the whole, unvarnished truth than an embittered drunk.

If Tanny noted the derision in Joe's voice, he didn't comment on it. Instead, he drained his drink and then slapped a twenty dollar bill on the bar and pushed it forward.

"Give me twenty, Joe," he said boastfully. "I think I'm gonna continue that lucky streak of mine."

Joe smiled sardonically as he pulled another beer. "How long that lucky streak been going on, Tanny?"

Tanny acted as if he didn't have a care in the world. "Since birth, boys. Since birth."

"Is that so?" Joe put the beer in front of Tanny

and then counted out twenty scratch-and-win lottery tickets from the roll that hung behind the bar. "There you go, Tanny. Hope you win a million."

"Chicken feed," said Tanny. He snatched up the coil of silvery cards and began dancing around the room, madly scratching at the lottery tickets.

Joe just shook his head as Tanny capered about while Rob, who hardly noticed what was going on, was still focused on the enigmatic Michael McCann.

"Hey, Tanny," said Rob. "That Michael McCann—his house is on a piece of your property, right?"

Tanny tossed away a dud lottery ticket and started scratching at another. He never took his eyes off them, but the question did register. "Yeah? So what?"

"Then he pays you rent, right?"

Tanny was still focused on his tickets. "Come on, baby . . . Shit!" He threw another losing ticket to the floor and stomped on it. "So he pays us rent, so what? Joe, give me my lucky scratcher."

Joe tossed him one of those little pink plastic bar straws. Tanny grabbed it and continued working on the film on the tickets.

Rob couldn't leave his particular obsession alone either. "So you must have some idea what goes on around McCann's house, right, Tanny?"

Joe rolled his eyes at both of the losers life had swept into his bar.

Tanny spoke through gritted teeth. "You know,

when I finally win this damn thing, there's going to be some big changes around here."

"Lemme guess," said Joe, "you're gonna build a library, right?"

Tanny shrugged. "Why not? Sounds good."

"Jody down at the bank says he doesn't even have a bank account," said Rob. "Never cashes a check. He must keep it all at home. He gets a pretty penny for that furniture of his. He never spends it on nothin'. I figure he's got a damn good stash in his mattress and every damn bit of it in cash."

"Shut up," suggested Joe.

The bartender didn't mind a little gossip, but speculation about the whereabouts of someone's valuables was not the kind of idle talk he welcomed in his establishment, particularly in front of a character like Tanny.

For a moment, Joe thought that Rob's words hadn't registered with Tanny, who was still engrossed in his lottery tickets. But Joe hoped in vain.

"Keeps his money at home, huh?" said Tanny. "Good for him. I keep mine at Morgan Stanley . . . and I dole it out to my beloved brother when I see fit."

"I'll bet he *really* appreciates that," said Joe.

"Hey," said Tanny lightly, "that was Dad's plan. Not mine. He set it all up before he died. If it was up to me, I'd give it all to Brother John right now."

"Uh huh," said Joe, playing along. "And how old was your brother when your dad died?"

"Twenty-two," said Tanny.

"And how old were you?"

"Thirteen."

Joe folded his arms across his chest. "Well, I guess that makes a lot of sense. Your father must have figured that two things that really go together are large fortunes and teenagers, right?"

Tanny had lost interest. He scratched his last ticket and his eyes lit up. He slapped it on the bar and crowed triumphantly. "Yes! There you go! I win."

"You win?" said Rob.

"Five bucks, my man. And I'll take it all *now*. No checks. Cash."

At that very moment, money was on Michael McCann's mind, too. He was still across the street in Mrs. Simon's cluttered shop, painstakingly examining a coin under a jeweler's loupe. It was a 1907 Liberty twenty-dollar gold piece, an uncommon, but not excessively rare coin. The real treasures, the unique coins of the past were beyond Michael McCann's wallet, but he was still an avid collector nonetheless. He wasn't interested in assembling a collection of rare coins, but in putting his hard-earned money into something secure, guaranteed, and immutable. Gold, as he had learned from Tommy Black, was permanent. There had already been far too much change in Michael's life, and he looked to his gold hoard to protect him, to secure him in one place, the way a weighty anchor allows a ship to ride out a heavy sea.

Good quality, pure gold coins of the early twentieth century were the best investment he could think of. Every time some money came his way at the completion of every project, he took his check down to Mrs. Simon's shop, ignored the antiques and the hoo-ha, and bought himself a coin. It was always the best he could afford, not the one with the most pleasing design or the most interesting history—it was the gold, not the story, that was immutable.

Mrs. Simon's business philosophy was not to stock the things she thought would appeal to others, but to merely buy the things *she* liked. Of course, given her rather curious outlook on life, she often got stuck with the more unusual items in her inventory, sometimes for years at a time. Still, she felt that if she hung on to something long enough, eventually *someone* would come along and take it off her hands.

All of this would suggest that Mrs. Simon was an eccentric, elderly woman, with long gray hair twisted into a tight bun, short-tempered, set in her ways, brusque with strangers, and unwilling to suffer fools gladly.

None of the above.

April Simon was pretty, thirty-five-years old, divorced, and mother of a three-year-old boy. She was carefree and casual, tolerant and forgiving to a fault. Also, she happened to be a shrewd judge of antiques, gems and jewelry, precious metals—and rare coins. While Michael examined the coin under the magnifying eyepiece, Mrs.

Simon talked. It wasn't a sales pitch, she was just making conversation.

"Nice coin, huh? The guy I bought it from wasn't kidding on the grade. I think you ought to get it."

All Michael could manage to say in reply was a noncommittal: "Hmmmm . . ."

She pointed to her latest hoo-ha acquisition, a large orange weather balloon draped in a corner of the shop. "How do you like that? Let me tell you, that is not going to be around here for long. Weather balloon collectors"—she shook her head in wonderment—"they are fierce. Once they get wind that I've got one, they'll be here ripping it off the walls."

Michael nodded and continued to study the Liberty twenty-dollar piece, taking in every detail.

"I guess the weather balloon people are a lot like the moose-head collectors in that respect, aren't they?" Michael said.

He straightened up and returned the loupe, but continued to hang on to the gold coin.

"Huh?" April Simon surveyed the half dozen or so motheaten moose heads scattered around her shop. They had been there a long time. "Oh, hell, never mind. I never understand half the things you're talking about."

"I think I'll buy this," said Michael McCann.

"It's a good buy. . . . Hey, come here. I want to show you something." She took him firmly by the elbow and walked him through the disorder in the front of the shop to a completely different world in the back room. Michael was amazed to see that April Simon's office was a high-tech communications center, with a bank of computers, fax machines, and scanners crowded on her large desk.

She slipped into her chair and typed rapidly, pulling up a coin collectors' bulletin board, a coast-to-coast numismatics market. April Simon searched through the entries on the screen.

"There's a guy on line with some uncirculated Walking Liberties. They have real potential, too, you know. Almost as good as the gold Liberties. Cheaper too." She scrolled through the information. "And I think he's in California so you wouldn't have to pay sales tax."

Michael shook his head curtly. "I'm not interested in silver," he said.

She hit a few more keys searching for the latest offering on the gold market. "Sorry, just getting the latest quotes. Checking on what's out there."

Michael's interest was piqued. The contrast between the front of the store and the back was pretty amazing. "You can do all that on there?"

April Simon nodded and smiled. "Honey, with this thing I can tell you the temperature in Singapore or the price of pork bellies in Barcelona. All with the touch of a button. But seriously, silver is good. Definitely worth thinking about a little. How come you're only interested in gold?"

Michael's words came to him automatically. He had said them to himself so many times that they came out like a mantra. "It's always there when you need it. It's the only thing that will never let you down."

Mrs. Simon thought this sounded unnecessarily bleak, but did not say so. Of course, in all of her dealings with Michael McCann, she had found him to be unfailingly gloomy and she, like everyone else in Burrows, wondered what great tragedy he kept so deeply hidden in his past.

Michael turned toward the door. "Thank you, Mrs. Simon. I had better get going."

"Jeez," she said under her breath. "Call me April. You've been coming in here for five years already."

Michael made for the office door quickly, acting as if he hadn't heard her—but he had, and even this small act of intimacy frightened him.

On impulse, April Simon jumped to her feet and chased after her taciturn customer. A sad man who trusted only in gold aroused both her pity and interest. Suddenly, she was determined to draw him out.

"I'm from Ohio," she called after him.

Michael stopped in his tracks, surprised as if he had suddenly been ambushed. He half turned. "Huh?"

"I'm from Ohio. Cincinnati," she said. "Where are you from? What town?"

He considered the question with the same wariness of an animal approaching a trap. "Why?"

"Just curious," she said with a shrug. "I mean, come on, you've been coming in here for five years and I don't know a thing about you."

Michael didn't like the question and it showed.

He walked a few steps toward the shop door, then stopped and turned. From somewhere within his soul a piece of the old Michael McCann appeared—the understanding, unfailingly polite man who had walked away from his old life so many years before. April Simon was just trying to be nice and he was acting like a churl—and he hated himself for it. He took a deep breath, like a diver about to take a plunge into an icy torrent.

"I'm from Washington, D.C." he said finally. He spoke like a man reading his own obituary.

Mrs. Simon smiled brightly. "See. Now that wasn't so bad, was it?"

A crooked, uncertain smile briefly crossed Michael McCann's lips, as if he hadn't quite mastered the mechanics of such an expression. Of course, she didn't realize what effort that trivial exchange had required.

Fresh from his victory beating the odds of the Virginia State Lottery, Tanny Newland strolled down the main street of Burrows. He was unwilling to go home just yet, and he didn't want to stay in the Rainbow being pestered by Rob's inane questions about the reclusive Michael McCann. He idled along, window-shopping and daydreaming, feeling pleasantly lightheaded from the two quick beers he had chugged down. In fact, it was probably the touch of alcohol in his veins that gave him the courage to do what he did next. Spying Daisy Lammeter in the clothing store where she worked, Tanny marched right in and started flirting.

"Can I help you?" she asked, the instant Tanny stepped across the threshold. She knew who he was, of course, and things were slow around the shop. It would pass the time to banter a bit with the great John Newland's younger brother.

"Do you sell men's clothes here?" He surveyed the racks and racks of skirts and blouses, the wall of high-heeled shoes, the cases of lingerie. . . . There was no way he could have mistaken the store for Brooks Brothers, but he was following the first rule of flirting: say anything, no matter how witless.

Daisy knew the rules, too—and she enjoyed flouting them. "No, no men's clothes here—but I'll measure your inseam if you want."

Whoa! thought Tanny. He laughed and pushed on, fingering a T-shirt on the nearest rack. "Uh . . . how much is this?"

Something like pity crossed Daisy's face. "Do you expect me to fall for that?"

Tanny always thought that he had a pretty smooth line with women, but Daisy was running rings around him. For a moment, he felt like some kid. He prayed that he hadn't flushed in embarrassment. Daisy moved swiftly, though, to put him at his ease.

"Sorry," she said. "I'm generally weirder than those around me. You're John Newland's little brother, aren't you? I was watching him play polo, not an hour ago."

"Yeah," said Tanny. "And he's *my* brother."

Daisy shook her head, understanding him perfectly. "Sorry," she said. "I should have known. I get that all the time, too. My sister is *the* Nancy Lammeter."

"I know the feeling."

"Tell you what," said Daisy. "Pick me up at nine-thirty tonight and we'll go out. You know how to dance, don't you?"

"You bet. I can dance like Frank Astaire himself," said Tanny grinning.

"I believe that's Fred. Fred Astaire," said Daisy.

"That's right," said Tanny. "I dance just like his brother Frank."

Daisy laughed loudly. "You know—"

"Yeah," said Tanny, "I know. I'm weird too."

3

The polo match was over, John Newland's team had won, the field was empty, the stands devoid of spectators, and now the real work began. In a quiet, secluded corner of the Burrows Hunt Club pavilion John Newland and Randy Keating sat facing two older men, Roy Strong and Len Hamilton, two back-room politicians who had driven all the way from Washington—but not just to watch John Newland play polo. Newland and Keating were still in their polo gear, Strong and Hamilton in shapeless, gray sack suits; only Keating looked uncomfortable.

"Coffee?" asked Strong.

"No thanks," said Newland.

"Wine?" offered Hamilton. "Something stronger?" It was plain that the politicians were speaking to Newland, and if Keating was thirsty that was just his tough luck.

"No thanks."

"Don't drink, John?" asked Roy.

Newland smiled a slight, knowing smile. "No need." He didn't think there was any point in telling them that once upon a time he had definitely had the need. John Newland, with that iron self-control, had cured himself of a serious drinking problem, a problem that would have drowned his political ambitions.

"You looked good out there," said Hamilton. He waved vaguely in the direction of the polo field. Again, it was obvious that he was not talking about the entire team but John Newland and John Newland alone.

Newland nodded as if taking his due. "Do you mean my playing or my campaigning?"

"Both," said Strong. That concluded the niceties as far as the pols were concerned. He hunched forward and spoke low. "You're a state representative. . . ."

"That's right."

"And I don't have to tell you that a state representative can get away with murder—literally. No one is paying any attention to you guys."

"Congress is a whole different ball game," put in Hamilton. "Once you get to Washington, people start paying attention."

"Tell me something I don't know, gentlemen."

Hamilton shook his head. "No. It doesn't work that way. You tell us."

"Tell you what?"

"I'll spell it out for you," said Strong. "The state level is small potatoes. But suppose you run for Congress and win, you make a nice splash in the House of Representatives. Suppose you do well and become senator. . . ."

"Senator Newland," said John, as if trying

out the title to see how it sounded. He nodded appreciatively. It sounded good, he had to admit.

"Well, Senator," Hamilton continued, "maybe we decide to run you for president."

"That would be nice," said Newland with a smirk.

"Well, if we're going to put any party money behind you, we want to know that if that time comes, you're clean."

"I'm clean." Newland's words were clipped and forceful. He didn't like anyone suggesting that he was anything less than perfect.

"Oh, yeah?" said Strong. "What about your brother? He strikes me as a little bit of an embarrassment. The kind of embarrassment that political parties—and candidates—can do without. Know what I mean?"

John Newland nodded, but mentally he catalogued the number of fraternal embarrassments that presidential candidates had endured over the years. Nixon, Carter . . . even Clinton.

It never occurred to Newland to be annoyed that two outsiders were calling a member of his family an embarrassment—the truth was that Tanny was a colossal pain in the neck *and* a constant source of embarrassment.

"I don't have to tell you, gentlemen, that embarrassing brothers don't lose elections. Do I?"

"Well, you can hardly call them an asset," said Strong sourly. "Can you control him?"

"Always."

Everyone had forgotten about Keating. He, however, was thrilled to be in on this conversation, to be privy to some real back-room politicking. Absentmindedly, he patted his pockets and pulled out a cigarette. The two politicians stared at him, as if unable to believe that anyone smoked anymore. Keating put the cigarette away. The smoke-filled room was plainly a thing of the past.

Strong almost whispered. "What about you, John?"

"What about me?"

"Anything serious we should know about?" asked Hamilton, hunching forward.

Newland nodded. "Yes, you should know this about me—I know that public office takes a special kind of will. But I am like a cannonball dropped from the top of Stone Mountain."

"Just what the hell does that mean?" asked Hamilton.

"It means that if something weak gets in my way, I go straight through it."

Strong and Hamilton exchanged looks, then smiled. They were liking what they were hearing.

"Anything else?" Newland asked.

"Any plans on getting married?" said Strong. "The voting public doesn't really trust single politicians." He rocked a hand from side to side. "They think it looks . . . you know, funny. The right wife can be an asset in public life."

"And the wrong one can be trouble," Newland retorted quickly. "I'm taking my time, but rest assured that a wife is definitely on the agenda."

Hamilton frowned. "Do me a favor—don't tell any jokes. They don't mix with politics."

John Newland laughed. "I give you my word. I will be extremely unfunny."

Strong thrust out his hand. "Shake on it."

By the time John Newland parked his Mercedes in the forecourt of his house that evening, his facade had begun to crack a little. He had much on his mind and was tired to boot. He was not happy to see a beaten-up Plymouth Duster drawn up by his own front door—this meant that his little embarrassment, his brother, Tanny, had come to call.

He strode into the house, the heels of his riding boots clicking on the marble floors. His irritation flared into anger when he discovered Tanny ensconced in his study, slumped on a sofa, his feet on the coffee table, drinking twelve-year-old scotch, and watching some trash on TV. Newland threw down his car keys and his polo helmet and glared at his younger brother.

"I thought I told you not to let yourself in," John Newland said coldly. "You have your own place. As I recall, there's a TV set in there, too. Unless you've pawned it, of course." It was the tone of voice that he would have used to reprimand an incompetent servant.

Tanny smiled. "Where is it written that you get the big house and I have to use the guest house?"

"I seem to remember reading it in Dad's will."

Tanny grinned wider. "Of course. That damned will." He shrugged. "Well, I had to let myself in. It was an emergency."

"An emergency?"

"Yes. I thought I smelled smoke."

"Very funny." Newland pushed by his brother and went to his desk, unlocked a drawer, and withdrew a sealed, pale blue envelope. He tossed it to Tanny. "Well . . . as long as you're here, you might as well make yourself useful."

Tanny scarcely glanced at the envelope. He weighed it in his hand for a moment, then slipped it into his jacket pocket. "There. See. You still need me a little bit, don't you." He picked up the bottle of Tulisker and slopped a little more into his glass.

"Let me use your car tonight. I'm going out for a while after I take care of your little business here." He patted his pocket, the one containing the envelope, and smirked knowingly at his older brother.

John Newland didn't hesitate. "No way."

Tanny sighed. "Okay. Now that we've gotten the predictable, knee-jerk answer out of the way, let me ask you one more time. How about loaning me your car tonight?"

"No way. It's too risky to take my car. It's noticeable. Take your Plymouth."

Tanny draped himself over the arm of the couch, as if leaning out of a car window. "Hey girls! Wanna go for a ride in my '84 Plymouth?" He doubted that Daisy Lammeter really cared what kind of car he drove, but that didn't stop him making a lunge for the car keys. But John's reflexes were not dulled by alcohol and he nailed Tanny, catching him by the wrist.

"I said *no*. By ten o'clock you'll be high as a

kite anyway and you won't care what car you're in and neither will the trash you're with.'' He pushed Tanny away and turned his back on him, as if he couldn't stand the sight of his dissolute younger brother.

''Listen to you,'' said Tanny nastily. ''A guy gets sober and all of a sudden he's Jesus.'' For a moment, he considered telling him that his date was *not* trash, but the sister of Nancy Lammeter, but he kept his mouth shut.

''Shut up,'' muttered John Newland. ''Shut your mouth.''

But Tanny wouldn't let it go. He taunted his brother like a child in a school yard. ''Daddy's boy. Wonderful Daddy's boy.'' He dug the blue envelope out of his pocket and waved it tantalizingly in John's face, just close enough to be annoying, but far enough to be out of reach. ''You wouldn't be so wonderful if everybody knew what I knew. Would you? Would you?''

For once, John Newland's anger got the better of him, overwhelming his truly astonishing powers of self-control. He lunged at his brother and slammed him into the wall, Tanny's head cracking into a mirror hanging there. John pushed his face up close to Tanny's.

''Don't threaten me, Tanny, don't even think about it. If I lose, so do you. And I know you're way too greedy to ever give it up. So, go get laid, go smoke dope, go be stupid. Just do it in a Plymouth.''

Tanny had drunk enough not to be scared. He fixed a mocking little sneer on his face and pulled the corners of his mouth down like a clown. "Sniff, sniff . . ." he said. "Whatever happened to brotherly love." He pulled away from his brother, rubbed the back of his head, and examined himself in the mirror, busily patting his ruffled hair back into place.

John Newland shook his head slowly, disgust registering plainly on his face. "Look at you, Tanny. How could anybody possibly love you?"

But Tanny wasn't listening. He was peering intently into the mirror, his fingers tracing a crack where his head had smacked into the glass. "Hey, Brother, a broken mirror. You know what that means, don't you?" Tanny smiled evilly. "Seven long years of bad luck."

4

Seventy-five miles and half a world away from Burrows, in a run-down part of Norfolk, Virginia, Marsha Swanson cooked a sticky lump of morphine in a blackened spoon, rendering the narcotic down into an oily liquid. Adroitly, she inserted the needle end of a hypodermic syringe into the fluid and sucked it up into the barrel of the device. Quickly, she tied off, cinching the veins of her bicep and began hunting for a vein in the crook of her arm, one that hadn't already been so perforated that it had collapsed. She found one, slipped the blunt, much-used needle into her flesh and shot the heroin into her blood stream. It only took a moment or two to blast through her, and she sagged and slumped forward, nodding as the warm security of the drug washed over her brain.

The girl's mouth was slack, but she managed to smile. For a while she could disappear into the drug, leaving behind her shabby world, forgetting the dirty, run-down welfare hotel room, the room she shared with a permanent mat of garbage, the roaches, her drugged-out boyfriend, Dwayne—and her daughter, one-year-old that day.

When she wasn't deadened with drugs, Marsha Swanson was rather a pretty girl, only eighteen years old. But her hard life of poverty and heroin had coarsened her, mottling her skin and making her formerly bright eyes bleary and dull. Her arms were scabbed and lacerated with needle tracks, and her skin hung loose on her slight frame as if the drug were eating her away from within. Her clothes were dirty and her makeup had been applied with an unsteady hand. Her nails were split and bloody where they had been chewed down to the quick.

The little girl on the floor next to her was a pure, fresh, miniature facsimile of her mother. Where Marsha's blond hair was thin and lank, the child's was soft and full. Marsha's blue eyes were cloudy, the child's as bright as clear water and sunlight, her skin as smooth and unblemished as fine velvet. They both had the same pert features, the turned-up nose, the wide red mouth, but there was a fire, an alertness in the baby that had been extinguished in the mother a long time ago.

Marsha scarcely looked up when the door of her room opened and Tanny entered. Back in Burrows, around the well-put-together blue bloods like his brother, Bryce and Keating, Tanny looked pretty shabby. In Marsha's dirty hovel, he appeared to have stepped from the pages of a men's fashion magazine. He took the envelope from his pocket and tossed it to her.

"Pennies from heaven," Tanny said. He picked up a half-smoked joint resting on the edge of a cracked and scorched table. "Hey, don't mind if I do." He lit it with his lighter and sucked the smoke deep into his lungs.

Marsha was more interested in the money. She tore open the envelope and pulled out three one-hundred-dollar bills.

"This is it? This is all?" She turned her hollow eyes on Tanny.

"I said *pennies* from heaven." He was sucking on the joint the way a tycoon puffs on a fine Havana cigar. There was nothing he enjoyed more than a well-rolled joint.

"Tell him we need more. Tell him his little girl needs more," Marsha said desperately. She put an emaciated arm around the child's shoulders.

"Mo' " said the little girl. The cheap silver charm bracelet on her mother's arm caught her attention and she thrust out her fingers to play with it.

"I do tell him, but doesn't do any good," he said, doing his best to sound sympathetic. "You know how he is. . . ." Tanny shrugged. He rather enjoyed having some power, even if he held it over an unfortunate piece of drugged-out human wreckage like Marsha Swanson.

Tanny did a quick turn around the dirty room, stopping to look at a snapshot of the little girl affixed to the refrigerator door with a magnet. He examined it closely, like a aesthete admiring a work of art in a posh gallery. The little girl looked cute, even in such threadbare circumstances. In the picture she was wearing the same red pajamas she had on right at that moment.

"How is wonder boy?" Marsha mumbled.

"Oh, he's swell," said Tanny sarcastically. "Everything's just great with the golden boy. Everybody thinks he's God." He winked broadly at Marsha. "But you and me, we know different, don't we, baby?" Tanny assumed she was too zonked to notice him whip the photograph from the refrigerator door.

The girl nodded. "We know different. We sure do. . . . Hey, don't take that, it's all I've got."

Tanny handed over the joint. "Sorry. I just wanted a little toot, that's all."

Marsha snatched the joint, but she shook her head. "Not that. The picture. That's the only picture I got of her." The child sensed her mother's distress and began to whimper, begging to be picked up and held.

"Look, I need it," said Tanny quickly. "I'll bring it back, I promise."

Through her drug-fogged brain, Marsha tried to figure out just what was going on. "What do you need it for? What are you gonna do with it?"

"I can get you more. You deserve more than this. He's rich, you know."

"That's not what he says."

"Take it from me," said Tanny. "He is richer than you think. He could help you—help you get out of this place. He could even help you kick, but he wants to keep you high to keep you quiet. Smack is cheap, you know?"

The child was squirming in her mother's lap, whimpering unhappily, tears beginning to form in her eyes. "There, there, baby," said Marsha, as soothingly as she could. "Don't worry. It's okay."

"Gotta go," said Tanny. He tapped the three hundred-dollar bills. "Invest it wisely." He hurried out of the room, almost running for his car. If he hustled, he could score a little dope on the Norfolk waterfront and still make it back to Burrows to meet Daisy more or less on time.

Marsha and Tanny weren't the only two people bent on obliterating reality that night—Michael McCann was going through his own nightly ritual of sedation.

His small drab house was closed up tight, the doors double locked and bolted, the thick curtains drawn, a single lamp burning. He was seated at his kitchen table, a bottle of cheap vodka and three shot glasses, a calculator, and a dog-eared copy of *Coin Dealer's Newsletter* arrayed before him like chess pieces. Slowly, methodically, he unscrewed the cap on the bottle and poured three generous doses of the clear, potent liquid into the glasses. He picked up the first and guzzled it down in a single gulp. As the liquid burned its way down his throat, Michael shuddered, as if absorbing a body blow.

The first part of the rite completed, Michael dug into his pocket and pulled out the gold coin he had purchased that day and held it before him, angling it toward the light until the coin glittered seductively. He reached under the table and retrieved a tattered piece of paper taped there and copied out the information on his new acquisition, carefully recording the date, condition, and the price he paid.

Now came his favorite moment. Michael had built the table he was sitting at and only he knew its secrets. Set into the top of the table was a hatch which slid back to reveal a deep, secret compartment. It was filled almost to capacity with gold coins.

There were hundreds of them: heavy American eagle fifty-dollar pieces, slightly smaller half eagles and fat, mill-edged double eagles—three ounces of pure gold. Some were tucked into plastic envelopes; others were loose-leaf coin pages. Some were stacked in tight rolls, each as heavy as a brick. Michael reached in and scooped up the coins and began putting them in neat stacks on the table.

Slowly, deliberately, he matched each coin against the updated value in the newsletter, entered it in the calculator, keeping a running total of his net worth as he worked. Midway through his collection, he stopped and slugged back the second shot of vodka, this one going down a little easier, as if the way had been smoothed by the path of gold. It took an hour or two for him to total up the whole collection, the final sum bringing a warm glow of pleasure.

Michael McCann had no particular love of or need for money. His wants were so rudimentary, so basic, that the amount of money he had hidden in his kitchen table could sustain him for years. He lusted after nothing, except security, and it was the protection and safety that the gold carried with it that mattered to him. It never occurred to him to dip into his hoard, even for essentials like new clothes or a better truck to replace the old rattle-trap he drove. The thought of real extravagance—a vacation, perhaps, or a dinner at an expensive restaurant—was completely beyond the bounds of reason. Even the vodka was the cheapest variety on the market. Michael consumed it not for taste, but for its ability to anesthetize him.

His only pleasures were his coins and his work. Work was a daytime activity, and he saved his miser's stockpile and his trio of vodka shots for the night. He picked up a pile of gold, Ben Franklin five-dollar pieces, a dozen of them, and rolled them in his palm. Then he divided them into two equal piles and shuffled them together with the dexterity of a card sharp at the top of his game, sighing happily as the coins slid smoothly through his fingers.

Then, with sadness, as if he were bidding goodbye to old friends, he replaced the coins in their dark little cabinet and closed them within the table top. He taped to the underside of the kitchen table the yellowed piece of paper with the tally of the coins' value—then he reached for the final glass of vodka.

Michael knew from years of practice that three shots of alcohol were enough to numb his brain, desensitize him to his horrible past and his barren future, and to give him the gentle push he needed to sink into a dreamless sleep. He slurped it down, scarcely noticing the burn now. Then he got up from the table and staggered to his bed. He fell onto it, and fully clothed, passed out. Another day done . . .

5

But that night was far from over. On the drive back from Norfolk, Tanny's booze-and-grass muddled brain had formulated a plan. The details remained to be worked out, of course—Tanny was never too strong on details—but the plan centered on the picture of Marsha's little girl, his brother's dirty little secret. The first part of the payoff would be the use of his brother's Mercedes for the night. The real compensation—some serious money in return for silence—he could negotiate later, at his leisure.

He got back to the Newland house in good time, despite the fact that a fog was coming in, and found his sainted brother seated at his desk in his study. He did not look at all happy to see Tanny.

"I'm surprised. I would have thought you'd be completely wasted by now," John Newland said sourly, scarcely looking up from the papers spread out in front of him. These were the position papers and strategy briefing books, the blueprint for his run for Congress.

"All in good time, Brother, dear. First things first." He thrust the photograph into John's hand and smirked. "Here you go, Dad. That ought to warm your heart." Then, as if not wishing to hang around to witness the touching scene, he dashed out of the room, neatly nabbing the keys to the Mercedes as he went.

If Tanny had expected any great remorse on the part of his brother, he would have been sorely disappointed. John Newland looked at the picture of his daughter coldly, as if she was nothing more than a stranger. Then he tore the picture into small pieces and threw them away, turning back to more important business—getting elected.

Daisy knew better than to be impressed by the sleek black Mercedes. She had seen Tanny rattling around town in his beat-up Plymouth, and she had seen his brother behind the wheel of the Mercedes. She had no doubt about who owned which car. Still, it was nice of Tanny to go to the trouble of borrowing a classy ride like that. It made her feel special, and dates that did that for her were few and far between.

It had been a long day for Tanny. He was tired and the long drive back from Norfolk, as well as the liquor and the hash he had ingested, already made him slightly unsteady behind the wheel. His inhibitions, though, were long gone.

"Well, babe," he said, "let's go dancing."

"Babe?" she said archly.

"Whatever." He reached into his jacket and pulled out a silver flask. "Drink?"

"What is it?"

"Fine Tennessee sippin' whiskey," he said with a grin. "Black jack."

Daisy shrugged. "Sure." She sipped and then handed the flask back.

"You know," said Tanny, doing his best to be charming, "I have a feeling it's going to be a wonderful night."

He drove out of town, making for a honky-tonk roadside nightclub just across the county line from Burrows. Showing off, Tanny put his foot down hard on the accelerator, the powerful car tearing a hole in the fog. But the mist was getting thicker and thicker, and the course the automobile carved in the fog was plugged in seconds.

Daisy wasn't scared, she was exhilarated. A fast car, a deserted country road with a nightclub at the end of it—these were definitely the makings of a good time, as far as she was concerned.

The joint they smoked in the honky-tonk parking lot was all part of the fun, too. No one had ever accused Daisy of being a Puritan.

The bar was just the way Daisy liked them: hot, crowded, noisy, rowdy—just this side of being dangerous and out of control. Daisy and Tanny had two beers each at the mobbed bar, then managed to elbow their way onto the crowded dance floor. The fiery music felt good, and the two fell into each other's arms, dancing close and hot, Daisy lithe and seductive against Tanny.

Tanny just let himself go. The music, the grass, the beers and the alluring body of his date combined to form a heady opiate and suddenly *every-*

thing felt good. He wasn't the derided little brother anymore—he was powerful. He had a beautiful woman in his arms, a fancy car outside, and, best of all, he had his brother right where he wanted him.

Despite the narcotic effects of the grass, the booze, and the great sex he sensed in his (very near) future, he hadn't forgotten his rancor against his brother. It would take a lot more than a couple of beers and a joint or two to erase that.

But now Tanny had John Newland right where he wanted him. And starting tomorrow, things would be changing around the Newland household.

But pleasure before business . . .

"Let's step outside," he whispered in Daisy's ear. "Let's get a little fresh air. . . ."

Daisy nodded and permitted him to take her hand and lead her toward the exit. The damp, cool air hit them with a wet slap, invigorating enough to take the edge off Daisy's drunkenness, but not nearly stimulating enough to cut through the haze in Tanny's brain.

The instant they were outside, he reached for her, jamming her against the side of the car and pawing her drunkenly. Daisy, of course, knew this was coming and was prepared to play along to a certain extent, but his kisses quickly turned sloppy, wet, and open mouthed, his tongue pushing past her lips, invading her mouth. His hands were all over her, and he pawed, grabbing at her breasts.

"Tanny . . ."

"C'mon, baby. C'mon." He panted in her ear and his breath was hot and intense. He reached between her legs and she broke free.

"Tanny! No!" She knew she was in no danger. She had handled drunks a lot tougher than Tanny Newland. It was his casual assumption that she was available that angered her, and she pushed him away.

But Tanny would not quit. He yanked open the door of the car and tried to drag her in, but Daisy wasn't going anywhere. She dug in her heels and pulled back. Then she broke free, backing away from him, snatching a broken brick from the ground, ready to clobber him with it if that was what was called for.

"Tanny! Back off, goddammit!"

"Okay . . . okay."

Her tone of voice suggested that there was little room for negotiation here and Tanny found himself sobering up a little. But not enough.

"Aww come on, Daisy. We were having a good time weren't we?" Suddenly, he didn't feel quite so powerful as he had a few moments before.

"Not anymore," she snapped. "Get me outta here. Now."

"Fine," he snarled. "Get in the goddamn car."

"Nothing funny," she cautioned. "Or I'll be forced to beat the crap outta you."

"Yeah . . . yeah," he grumbled, slipping in behind the wheel. He started the engine and gunned it a couple of times. But before he took off, he turned to her, willing to try one last time.

"Daisy," he drawled, hoping he sounded conciliatory, "look . . . why don't we forget about it? Go back inside, have a few drinks, some laughs, you know. . . ."

Daisy stared back at him for a moment. Then: "Drive," she said.

"Goddammit!" He slammed the car into gear and peeled out of the parking lot, moving fast, leaving a wide stretch of hot rubber on the asphalt. The Mercedes performed up to specification, going from a standing start to sixty miles an hour in a matter of a few short seconds.

Even at the best of times and under the best of conditions, Tanny would have been driving too fast. But pushing a powerful, high performance car through the fog along winding, dark country roads, under the influence of drugs, alcohol, and a steaming head of anger—this was a recipe for disaster.

And a disaster was not long in coming.

He took a tight turn at top speed and didn't have time to react to the two large boulders that had tumbled into the road from the slope above the highway. The car bounced over the rocks, a sickening tearing sound scraping along the underside of the vehicle. There was a shower of sparks and the heady stink of gasoline pouring from the ruptured gas tank.

"Tanny!" screamed Daisy, "Look out!"

There was a bang as loud as a shotgun blast as one of the tires blew out, the car swerving crazily to the left. The wheel was stiff and didn't respond to his frantic attempts to yank the car back on course.

Everything was happening fast, and curiously, in a detached sort of slow motion. Far off, Tanny could hear Daisy screaming—or was she swearing—but all he could think was: *My brother is going to kill me. . . .*

The car skidded off the road, crossed the shoulder, and slammed nose first into a tree. For a second, the bright silver cushion of the air bag blasted into his face, obscuring his vision—a lucky break for him as he was spared the horrible sight of Daisy smashing full force into the windshield. The crack of her head against glass was a sickening sound which seemed to cut through the scream of the racing engine.

Tanny was fine, saved by the air bag, but he was sweating from the pulse of adrenaline pumping through his body. Daisy was slumped over in the leather bucket seat, her face a mask of blood. She was lying very still.

"Goddamn," he muttered. "Goddamn. Goddamn." The adrenaline fought the pot and the booze in his brain as he desperately tried to control his panic. He fumbled for her arm, pulling at her slack wrist, frantically searching for a pulse, praying for any sign of life.

As the full, awful impact of what had happened began to sink into his fuddled brain, he felt sick to his stomach, more scared than he had ever been before. Tanny's life was really nothing more than a succession of mishaps, some serious, most trivial. He had lied, he had stolen, he would cheat at cards if he thought he could get away with it.

But basically, he was harmless. In his long career of screwing up, he had never *killed* anybody. . . .

But now he had. He closed his eyes and imagined what the future held. The cops, a trial, the publicity . . . *jail*!

He wiped the sweat from his upper lip.

"Jesus," he whispered, "I need a drink." Then, happily, he remembered the flask in his jacket pocket. He yanked it out and drank down the bourbon as if it was cold spring water.

Tanny staggered out of the wreckage of the Mercedes and stumbled down the road. Getting out of there wasn't good enough—he had to disappear and for a long time, and that meant money, a lot of it. As usual, his bank account was running on empty, and he had tapped out every possible source of a loan. His only hope was his brother. Cold comfort.

"Oh, shit." He closed his eyes and took another pull on his flask and said a little prayer that this was nothing more than a horrible nightmare.

He would have to throw himself on John's mercy, beg him for money to get away. Tanny swallowed more of the liquor and for a moment managed to con himself into thinking that John would help him get away, give him money. With his resources and connections John Newland would shield his brother, get him out of the country until the storm blew over. After all, Newland couldn't afford a scandal. An embarrassing brother was one thing; having one who was a murderer was another altogether. . . .

Maybe John could hush the whole thing up.

He could say that the car had been stolen, that someone else had cracked it up, that—Tanny's hopes evaporated instantly, as cold reality came crashing in like a breaker.

A dozen people had seen him with Daisy at the bar and besides, John would rather throw him to the wolves than to stick out his precious neck. *He* could weather the storm, but Tanny would go down for the count.

Tanny was off the road now, stumbling blindly through a thicket of woods, lost in the fog. He had not the slightest idea where he was or where he was going. When he stopped to try and get his bearings, the thick mist swirled around him like a shroud, and the only sound he could hear was the heavy pant of his tortured breathing and the frantic hammering of his heart.

He took another swig from the flask and tried to calm his hysterical nerves. Then, as if the waters had parted, there was a break in the fog, and in the darkness Tanny could make out the murky outline of the rundown house of Michael McCann. In a rush, Rob's words came back to him: *I figure he's got a damn good stash in that mattress and every damn bit of it in cash.* And right then, cash, a lot of it, was just what he needed.

Michael McCann's little house had stood on the Newland property for almost a hundred years, and Tanny had dim memories of exploring the house when he was a child, playing in the musty corners, and clambering in the rickety rafters. He even recalled that it was in the old shack that he had drunk his first six pack one spring afternoon, many years before, when playing hooky from the ninth grade. Maybe he would remember his way around.

Tanny peered through one of the windows and could just make out the figure of Michael stretched out on his bed. His mouth was open and he was snoring slightly, sleeping peacefully. All Tanny had to do was be silent and be careful, get the money, and get out. He knelt and felt around on the damp ground until his hand closed around a rock. Tanny had no stomach for violence. Deep down he knew himself to be a coward, but that night he knew he would not hesitate to bash in McCann's head if he had to.

One of the small panes of glass in the front door was cracked, and it was a simple matter for him to remove the shard of broken glass, slip the locks, and step inside, the fog billowing in behind him.

The rock in his hand, he walked toward Michael, ready to attack the sleeping man if necessary. But then he caught sight of the vodka bottle and the three shot glasses still standing on the kitchen table. This reassured Tanny. He himself was no stranger to vodka hangovers, and he knew that if Michael had drunk enough, then he would sleep through the second coming, never mind a simple breaking and entering.

Tanny began skulking around the house, peering into all the obvious hiding places: in cabinets and cookie jars, behind the few books on the shelves, and in every nook and cranny of Michael's overflowing tool bench. Nothing.

Just then the wind blew through the house, wood shavings and dust balls scuttling before the cold air. The door creaked on its rusty hinges and Tanny froze, glancing worriedly toward the bed. But Michael did not stir.

The second gust caught the piece of paper, the one taped to the underside of the kitchen table, and pulled it loose. Hanging by a single strand of tape, the paper fluttered gently in the breeze for several seconds before Tanny noticed it.

The moment he laid eyes on the list, he knew what it was. The figures scrawled there made his heart race. Michael McCann had stored up more than enough to allow Tanny to disappear and to do it in style.

Visions of blue water, warm beaches, and even warmer girls swum through his head and he almost threw himself on the table, searching for the secret compartment. His probing fingers swept across the top, feeling for the fine join.

Tanny forced his nails into the crack, pulled the top off the table—and his mouth dropped open. The cache of coins was truly a breathtaking sight, the pile of gold an astonishing vision of riches, particular when viewed in contrast with the mean and miserly surroundings of Michael McCann's drab little house.

His heart racing, Tanny snatched a plastic bag from the kitchen counter, and almost diving into the little space, started slinging the coins into the sack. It only took a moment or two to strip the secret compartment. It was time to go. Tanny paused only to snatch the vodka bottle from the table, and without so much as a glance in Michael's direction, he tottered out of the house and into the fog, staggering under the weight of his ill-gotten treasure and the sudden explosion of vodka in his stomach. In a moment or two he had vanished, wraithlike, into the dark and foggy night.

The house stood silent. Michael McCann sprawled on the bed, slumbering through the last few moments of a calm and dreamless sleep. It was his last refuge and the last period of calm he would know for years to come.

The wind blew, the old door creaked on its joints, then, catching the breeze swung shut, slamming loud and hard, shaking the flimsy walls. Michael awoke with a start and a snort, rubbing his eyes and aware, vaguely, that something was not as it should be. He was cold, his cabin full of frosty, damp night air. With some effort, he swung out of the bed, groaning slightly as the full weight of his hangover pounded in his forehead, and blundered toward the open door.

Then he saw the table, and the sight of the empty hole made his heart leap violently. He fell on it, shoving his hands into the compartment, searching every corner of the niche and finding nothing but the perfect joins of his own carpentry.

For five or ten long, tortured seconds he struggled to comprehend what had happened, but the thought that his gold was gone just *couldn't* form in his mind. All he felt was terror and the eager effort to put an end to that terror. For a moment he convinced himself that his eyes deceived him, that this was a terrible liquor-induced nightmare. But he was awake and the gold was not in its hiding place.

Michael put his hands to his pounding head and tried to think. Had he put his coins somewhere else, and in his drunkenness forgotten his new hiding place? Like a man possessed, he dashed around his small house, searching every corner, sweeping his tools from his bench, even overturning his bed, shaking it and kneading the mattress between his trembling fingers. Then, in despair, he dug around the secret compartment again, exploring there for the last time.

But it was empty. Every last coin had vanished. Michael sank down on his knees and folded his arms around his head, rocking from side to side, trying to subdue the pain that flashed through his entire body, hot and fierce, as if he was being broken on a torture wheel.

He shook his head slowly and tears started in his eyes. Why did life persist on stealing from him all that he held dear?

6

This was a night they would talk about for years to come around Burrows, particularly in Joe's Rainbow Bar where the second act of the evening's drama would be played out.

The Rainbow was never crowded and that foggy evening was no exception. Rob was there, sitting at one of the back booths with some truckers he knew, and Joe was at his usual station at the bar. The only other customer in the joint was the Burrows's chief of police, a kindly, portly guy named Hubert, but whom everyone called Dad. He was kicking around one of the town's perennial favorite subjects: the history and probable future of Burrows's first and most prominent family, the rich folk with the big house up on the hill, the Newlands. Of course, it was fitting that he was telling his tales in the Rainbow Bar, the tavern being something of an unofficial shrine to the Newland family. Tanny was a regular. And John Newland, in his drinking days, had made the Rainbow the setting for some of his most famous, uproarious escapades.

"I was there when John and Tanny Newland's mom and dad were married," he told Joe. "Strangest wedding I ever saw."

"That so?" said Joe. "What made their wedding stranger than anybody else's?"

Dad laughed. "Well, I'll tell ya. . . . So the bride walks down the aisle, right, all nice and formal. Mr. Newland waiting at the altar. Everything just the way you'd expect a Newland wedding to be. Even had nice weather, like the Newlands had ordered it up specially, you know."

Joe nodded. Everything always seemed to work out well for the Newland family—except for Tanny, of course, but every family had to have a black sheep.

"And then the preacher says to Mrs. Newland 'Wilt thou have this man to be thy wedded wife?' And she says yes."

"Really?" said Joe with a broad grin.

Dad nodded vigorously. "Absolutely. But it gets weirder. *Then* the preacher says to Mr. Newland, 'Wilt thou have this woman to be thy wedded husband?' And Newland says, 'I do.' Nobody notices this but me and they go on like nothing happened."

"And who ended up wearing the pants in that family?" asked Joe.

Dad cackled. "Well, he did, as it turns out. The hell of the thing was—"

And that was as far as he got, because in that very moment Michael McCann burst into the bar, blundering in out of the foggy, eerie night, looking as weird as a werewolf. His eyes were wild, his hair seemed to be standing straight up.

Joe almost jumped out of his skin. "What the hell?"

Rob and his trucker friends sat stock-still, their beer tankards half raised to their lips.

"Where's the police?" Michael wailed.

"Right here," said Dad. "Don't panic."

Michael looked around, his deranged eyes boring into the few patrons of the Rainbow. "Was it you?" He jabbed a bony finger at Rob. "Was it any of you?"

"What the hell you talking about?" Joe demanded. "What's going on here?"

"Goddamn it! I've been robbed!" It was the first time he had actually spoken the words and the crushing realization of what had befallen him struck him like an iron bar across his back. He clutched at his head and groaned miserably.

Rob watched this whole performance unmoved. "Robbed?" he whispered. "And murdered, too."

The beefy policeman swung off his barstool and hiked up his belt. "Well, you don't have to go accusing any of us. Come on, we got three cars out there doing nothing. We'll catch 'em." He strode out of the bar to his cruiser and fired up the radio, calling the police cars in the field.

It didn't take long to move the entire Burrows's police force out to Michael McCann's place. The six-man force scoured the area but found nothing except for an empty bottle of cheap vodka and a few muddy footprints. They followed them as far as they could, before they petered out in thick brush.

They did, however, find the wrecked Mercedes and Daisy Lammeter. She was not, as Tanny had thought, dead, but seriously injured. The town ambulance rushed her to the hospital.

Watching the ambulance scream away in the night, Dad shook his head. "You know, all we need is a fire and we'll have used every piece of emergency machinery the town's got tonight."

Of course, there was only one black Mercedes in Burrows, and it wasn't long before John Newland was roused from his bed. No one ever assumed, not even for a moment, that he had anything to do with the accident or the theft of Michael's coins. Even before Daisy Lammeter regained consciousness, all the clues were pointing directly at Tanny Newland.

All the commotion around town had been picked up on the police scanners that ran twenty-four hours a day in the offices of the *Burrows Bugle* and it wasn't long before a reporter was on the scene.

By the time the reporter got back to the paper and wrote his story, John Newland was already huddled with Cal Mosely, the editor, engaged in some very active spin doctoring.

"The police are saying that after the accident, Tanny left the girl for dead."

"Bastard," whispered Newland.

"Well, I left that out of the story for now," said Mosely, doing his best to be reassuring. "Then, it seems, he stumbled on to McCann's house, robbed him, and then hightailed it out of town. He probably wasn't injured because there was an air bag on the driver's side . . . and there wasn't any blood around McCann's house."

"Are they sure Tanny did the robbery?"

"Well, the police seem pretty convinced, John," said Mosely soberly.

"And McCann didn't have any insurance, did he?"

"What do *you* think?"

John Newland shook his head slowly. "No, I guess not. . . . Where's Tanny now? He's not smart enough to pull this off."

"Well, he's made a pretty quick getaway," said Mosely. "There's no trace of him anywhere. He must have come out of the accident okay."

Newland nodded gravely. That was his brother all over. "No, he wouldn't have hurt himself," he murmured. "He likes to hurt others."

7

Daisy Lammeter's injuries were severe, but she would recover. The blow to her spirit had been brutal as well, but that too was on the mend. Swathed in bandages and plaster, scarcely able to move in her hospital bed, she did her best to smile at her sister.

"That was one of the worst dates I've ever been on," Daisy said. She looked terrible, with deep purple bruises under each of her eyes—the result of her broken nose. Her voice was rough, throaty, and dry.

"*One* of the worst?"

"I have the most terrible taste when it comes to men, Sis, you should know that by now." Daisy grinned and then winced. "It only hurts when I laugh."

"Don't laugh," Nancy advised.

"I know," said Daisy, nodding. "This is serious. Tanny is in deep trouble, I guess."

"He would be if they could find him."

"Well, for once it's not me in hot water. It's a funny feeling . . . strange."

"Maybe you could get to like it," said Nancy. "It's not the worst thing in the world, you know."

Daisy nodded. "I'm thinking of going back to school," she said solemnly.

"That's a terrific idea, Daisy." Nancy could hardly believe what she was hearing. Her sister had always had a strong aversion to classrooms, chalk, books, and anything else associated with education.

"Well . . . I figured if I'm going to meet jerks, I might as well be getting an education."

The two women didn't know whether to laugh or cry. They ended up doing a little of each. . . .

John Newland was outside, standing by Nancy's car in the hospital parking lot, patiently waiting for her to emerge from visiting her sister. It was not in Newland's psychological makeup to feel much in the way of guilt and he certainly wasn't going to take the blame for his brother Tanny's disastrous conduct. Still, he felt that something had to be put right between the Newlands and the Lammeters. He had his reasons.

Nancy saw John the moment she came through the door, and she walked quickly toward her Honda, her head bowed and her eyes down, as though she hoped that when next she looked up, John Newland would have vanished. She did not get her wish.

"Nancy . . ." said John Newland, walking toward her, "please wait a moment."

Nancy stopped and faced him, her arms folded across her chest, anger in her eyes. "Well?"

"I'd like to talk to you," said Newland. "It would be important to me."

"Not to me," she said curtly, and tried to push past him, but he blocked her path.

"Nancy," he said, "your 'no' has always been a pretty loud 'yes' to me."

This stopped Nancy dead in her tracks, her mouth open. Then she shook her head as if she couldn't quite believe he had said the words. "That is the most arrogant thing I have ever heard. That is egotistical even for you, John Newland. Which is really saying something."

He smiled, amused by her irritation. "Everyone has an ego, Nancy. I'm up-front about mine, that's all. That's not so hard to understand, is it?"

Nancy Lammeter did not want to have this conversation, so she continued to walk toward her car, digging in her purse for her keys. John Newland trailed after her.

"You leaving town soon?" he asked.

"Looks like I'll be here 'til Christmas now."

Newland nodded. "That's good."

"Have they managed to locate your brother yet? Or did he slip through the net?"

John Newland shook his head in disbelief. "It's amazing. Tanny is usually such a screw up, but it looks like he beat the odds this time."

"Where would he go?"

"He always talked about going to South America. . . . Now that he has some money maybe he decided to head south of the border. Of course, he'll run out of money eventually and I doubt he'll pull off another score like McCann's. *Then* he'll swim back into my life. I think I've got a collect, crackly phone call somewhere in my future."

"Lucky you," Nancy said sourly.

"I'm sorry," he said. "I didn't mean to joke. . . . It was my brother's destiny to hurt someone. I'm sorry that person was your sister."

Nancy turned and faced him head-on. "I'm a levelheaded girl, John. I don't blame you for what happened."

John Newland nodded and smiled softly. "Good. That's what I needed to know."

"Bullshit," said Nancy.

It wasn't every day that John Newland was taken completely by surprise. "What?"

"Look," said Nancy, pointing into the street. John Newland turned and saw two children, a boy and a girl, both about ten years old. They were busily pedaling their bikes down the street—and wearing small cardboard boxes on their heads. It was an absurd, but amusing sight and Nancy and John found themselves sharing a smile.

"That's life for you," said Newland. "In the midst of all this *trouble*, you see two kids with cardboard boxes on their heads."

Nancy nodded. "John, I don't think I'm pretty. I may be, but I don't think about it—"

"You are," John Newland insisted.

"Let me finish."

"Sorry."

"I don't think I'm pretty, but I do know I'm desirable or we wouldn't be standing here would we?"

Straightforwardness was something John Newland admired and he found it refreshing in a woman like Nancy Lammeter. "No," he said, "I guess we wouldn't."

"I only know you as the man who drove his car into the plate-glass window of the Rainbow Bar, rolled down his window and said 'Another.' "

John Newland looked suitably embarrassed, disconcerted to be reminded of an event from his wild youth. "That was a long time ago."

"Yes, but people remember, and I guess that sort of thing is pretty funny among the boys. The boys probably think it's pretty funny that you're the guy who tried to have every girl in town, including me." She shook her head and smiled knowingly at him. "I don't know if your womanizing was just reckless youth or a sickness."

"You're being so unkind you're turning me on," said Newland with a laugh. "Look, Nancy, I'm a different guy now. I can be politically correct till your sorority pin rots. Trust me. It's true."

"Oh, yes? And how long ago was it when you told me my 'no' meant 'yes'? I don't say things I don't mean. Not unless I'm lying, of course."

"I saw you smile when I said it."

"I smiled at the pure brass of it," Nancy protested. "I don't think you want that line quoted in the Congressional Record. I'll tell you what—I'll do you a favor and I won't tell anyone. *Now* don't accuse me of being heartless."

"I won't," said John. "Maybe you should be my campaign manager."

"Careful," she said with a smirk. "I don't think you'd like that. I thought Nancy Reagan was too weak."

"There must be something about me you like."

"Oh, yes," she said evenly. "There's something I like about you. I like it very much."

"Let me guess . . . it's my boyish charm, isn't it?" He flashed his most dazzling smile.

She shook her head. "No, it's not that. It's your success I respect."

Nancy had gone beyond straightforwardness. Now she was being blunt. John Newland liked that, too.

"My success? I haven't had it yet. I have to win the election first."

"If you do," Nancy said briskly, "let's talk. Meet me at Starbucks and I'll buy you a cup of black coffee. You look like you need it." She turned and walked toward her red Honda, then stopped and turned back.

"By the way," she said. "I also find you attractive."

In due course, John Newland announced his run for Congress and spent a hard couple of months campaigning for office and for the attention of Nancy Lammeter. In both endeavors, Newland scored his customary success. By election day, he had his Congressional seat more or less sewn up and he was seeing Nancy every day. They were together so much that it seemed that she was becoming the unofficial companion of the candidate.

Nancy was at John Newland's side at the victory celebration Newland threw a party for the bigwigs who supported his candidacy, as well as the faithful who had worked for him turning out the vote, and gotten him elected. Hundreds of people from around the state had been invited and John Newland's servants were out in force, along with the off-duty cops acting as security, and the car parkers. Both the police and the parking valets had unenviable assignments, working out-of-doors, as the night was bitterly cold, and made worse by an icy, frigid west wind. A thick layer of snow blanketed the frozen ground.

A few of the guests had brought their children with them, but they were given over to the care of April Simon, specially hired for the evening as baby sitter in chief.

All his life John Newland had been waiting for this night, and now that it was here, he seemed removed from it, less involved in celebrating his own success than he would have imagined he would be. What interested him most right then was Nancy Lammeter. In the middle of the party, among all his guests, he went up to her and whispered in her ear.

"If I could, I would cook you and eat you."

"Have a canape instead," she stage-whispered. Then she smiled brightly at one of the guests. "Hello, Judge Marcus. I'm Nancy Lammeter."

Judge Marcus was a heavy-set, elderly man with a bristly walrus mustache. Even though he was the leading magistrate in the county, he was immensely surprised and flattered that such a pretty girl would recognize him.

"You know my name?"

"I studied *Johns* versus *Dobson* in college, Judge Marcus. A landmark case—you made our little town into a big one," she said.

Marcus laughed heartily. "That case was a long time ago. I'm amazed anyone even bothers with it now."

"You'd be surprised, Judge Marcus."

John watched her closely, studying how she handled herself and the way other people responded to her. He liked what he saw. Nancy was self-assured, at ease with other people, and they always responded to her, pleased that they had attracted her attention. In short, she would make a perfect political wife.

She could even handle drunks. One of John Newland's merriest supporters, so delighted that Newland had been elected that he got himself completely inebriated, lurched over and studied Nancy closely. He pointed an unsteady finger at her and spoke with the exaggerated aplomb of the very intoxicated.

"I have to admit, I am intrigued. Very, very intrigued," he said.

John was quick off the mark, deflecting the drunk's interest easily. "Gosh," he said, "that's funny. Because I'm intrigued, too. Are you intrigued, Nancy?''

Nancy only hesitated a moment. ''Absolutely. Yes, I am very intrigued.''

John nodded. ''Well, I guess that settles it. We're all intrigued. And I have to thank you for stopping by and letting us know.'' Adroitly, he steered Nancy away from the man, leaving him puzzled, but without hurt feelings. It was an admirable skill for a politician. The next time the drunk got a fund-raising letter from John Newland, he would remember his intriguing conversation with his congressman and give generously.

''Now you have to admit that I'm better than that guy,'' John whispered.

''Okay,'' she said laughing, ''I admit you're better than that guy. Satisfied?''

''So what are you going to do?'' he asked, suddenly turning serious.

''What do you mean?''

''Are you going to be leaving? You said you'd be going back to school after Christmas.''

Nancy shook her head slowly. ''I don't know . . . I think I should stay with Dad and help with Daisy. But these days, you need a law degree to work at McDonald's. Law degrees are like opinions—everybody's got one. So, I'm going back to school. Not right away, but I will eventually.''

''Tell me, is that before sleeping with me or after sleeping with me?''

Nancy met his smirk with a cool, steady gaze.

"There's something you should know about me before this conversation goes any further. Something you might not want to hear."

"I want to know everything about you," he said, ever the flirt. "Especially if it's a deep dark secret from your sordid past."

"It's no secret," she said "It's very simple. If I sleep with you, I don't go back."

"Don't go back," he said. "Stay with me."

Her eyes were bright and she felt the warm sensation of love flooding through her. She was about to answer when the front door of the house was flung open and a gust of cold air flooded through the room.

Standing in the doorway was a man, a large bundle in his arms. It took Nancy a moment or two to recognize Michael McCann. His eyes were wild, his hair matted on his head, his shoulders dusted with fresh snow.

Suddenly, the room was suffused in silence, every one of the party goers frozen in place. His eyes swept over them, burning with intensity and anger. His gaze brought as much chill to the room as the rushing wind.

The blanket in his arms fell, revealing a tiny head and two shining eyes. Then, in the sepulchral voice of an Old Testament prophet Michael McCann spoke.

"Does anybody know this child?"

8

Tanny Newland had not been a man upon whom life had settled very many responsibilities, but he did have one. In the months since he had disappeared, no one had visited Marsha Swanson with her envelope full of hush money. Paltry though John Newland's payoffs may have been, they were Marsha's principal means of support and not receiving her payments had made life for her and for her little girl, already difficult, even more arduous.

Her drug habit had to be supplied. The relentless craving for heroin was always the first need to be met, even at the expense of food or warm clothing for the child. But Marsha's access to cash was limited.

She had no job so she had to rely on what she could steal, beg or earn through occasional and casual prostitution. But she was not a very accomplished thief and her bedraggled, strung-out looks meant that she could only attract customers scarcely less desperate than Marsha herself.

Dwayne, her boyfriend, was little help. He

was marginally better at larceny, but he resented sharing his money or his heroin. Marsha was more likely to get a punch than anything else from him.

Bad drugs, hard living, malnourishment, and constant worry were taking their toll on Marsha. Her health—already precarious—was breaking down. The apartment was cold and damp, and Marsha had developed a deep cough that racked and shook her body. Her little girl was thin and drawn, shivering in the cold, with nothing warm to wear except for her threadbare pajamas covered with the little red hearts.

Daily, mother and daughter awaited the arrival of the moneyman, but Tanny, of course, never showed up. Like a guttering candle, their hope burned low and, finally, went out.

Strangely enough, news of John Newland's election did penetrate the gloom of the squalid apartment. Rummaging in a Dumpster, Marsha had found a copy of that day's newspaper and the election of her former lover was splashed prominently on the front page, including a picture of a smiling John Newland standing on the front steps of his grand house in Burrows. This bit of information was enough to galvanize Marsha out of her lassitude. She showed the newspaper to the little girl.

"That's your father," she said. "You wanna go see your father?"

The little girl just looked at her, her big blue eyes uncomprehending.

"You'd like that, wouldn't you?" Marsha

thought for a moment. "I bet *he'd* like that." And she allowed herself a little laugh, imagining John Newland's embarrassment, his absolute mortification, if suddenly, his little family appeared at his grand front door.

The little girl laughed, too, and reached up and touched her mother's face. But the innocent, loving gesture irritated Marsha and she slapped the little hand away. The child flinched and recoiled, her blue eyes clouding and filling with fear. Instantly, Marsha was overcome with remorse and she reached down and gathered the child up in her arms.

"I'm sorry, sweetie," she said, cooing in her little one's ear and stroking her soft hair. "I'm so sorry. Mommy's not feeling too good tonight."

The baby burrowed farther into Marsha's arms, crying miserably, her gaunt little body shaking as she wailed. She raised her face to her mother and cried, a cold, hungry, miserable little creature.

"There, there, baby. There, there," she said, trying her best to calm her little girl. "Here we are, honey. All alone. Just the two of us. . . . It's gonna be all right. You'll see, honey, you'll see."

The little girl was pacified a little bit, but she continued to weep softly.

"What's Daddy doin' tonight, honey," Marsha cooed, as if singing a lullaby. "What's Daddy doin?" Even though her brain was clouded with drugs and drink, Marsha could imagine John Newland well enough to conjure up his handsome face. Where was he? He was secure and warm, with plenty to eat and drink. He was in a safe place, a world away from the squalor to which he had condemned his little girl.

"He's forgotten about his little girl," Marsha moaned. "He's forgot about you, like you never existed. He shouldn't have done that. He shouldn't have forgotten about his little girl."

Marsha stood and wrapped the child in a dirty blanket. "It's time to make him remember." She retrieved the car keys from the hiding place in the kitchen cabinet, gathered her baby up in her arms, and went out into the cold night.

The beat-up, ten-year-old Chevrolet parked in the dirty alley behind their tenement building didn't react well when she turned the key. The engine growled and wailed, but on the third try, it grumbled into life, running hot and ragged. The fuel level was low, but Marsha had no money for gas. All she could do was hope she had enough fuel to make it all the way to Burrows.

Marsha's nerves were jangled and she hadn't driven for a long time. The car lurched down the highway, barreling into the teeth of a worsening snowstorm. Marsha's driving was erratic and dangerous, and it was the bad weather that saved her from being pulled over. State troopers were laying low until the storm had blown itself out.

It took a couple of hours, but Marsha did manage to plow through the blizzard to the outskirts of Burrows. Then the car gave out, rolling to halt on the dark, cold country road. The Chevy died only a few hundred yards from the place where John Newland's Mercedes and Tanny's fortunes had taken such a disastrous turn a few months before.

When the car died, Marsha sat for a moment, hot tears starting in her eyes. The snow was caking against the windshield and the wind whipped through the night. She wasn't sure she could go on. . . .

"Mommy?" The little girl's eyes were filled with apprehension. "Sleepy . . . I'm sleepy."

"Okay . . . okay." Marsha collected what remained of her stamina. "We have to walk, honey. It's not far. . . . C'mon, baby, I'll carry you."

The cold was intense and cut through their thin clothes and inadequate shoes in an instant. Head down, Marsha struggled into the wind, her little girl enfolded in her arms, her head resting just under her chin. Each step was unsteady, the cold driving into her body like ten penny nails, draining her of her small store of strength.

They covered a mile or so, battling forward a few feet at a time. Marsha kept repeating the same words over and over as if they gave her strength to keep going on.

"Daddy said he would rather die than marry Mommy," she muttered. "Said he would rather die."

They battled on, staggering a few hundred more yards, but Marsha could feel exhaustion beginning to sap her, each step became torture and her cough, constant now, was tearing her apart with the pain. She stumbled against a snow bank and fell to her knees, dropping the child to the cold ground.

Marsha was panting now, fighting for every breath, tears streaming from her eyes. "I'm sorry, honey," she whimpered. "I'm sorry. I can't carry you anymore." She took her child's little hand and they trudged a few more feet. But Marsha's fragile body, beaten down by years of abuse, was already worn out. She had to stop. She had to stop and rest.

She realized now that they never should have left the car and the little shelter it would have afforded them, but there was no hope of their fighting their way back to it. Marsha staggered to a tree and leaned against it. Then her legs gave out and she sank into the snow, trying to envelope the little girl in her arms, to give her some protection from the wind.

"We'll wait here, honey," she said, her words were slurred and her voice low and indistinct. Her eyes were drooping shut. Fatigue gripped her like tight iron bands, and she could hardly feel the cold anymore. "We'll wait here until the snow stops falling."

It took only a matter of seconds for the blessed release of numbness to steal over Marsha. Her head slumped forward on her chest, her breathing shallow and strained. Not even her deep coughs could awaken her.

They were in a dense wood, deep and still, but the little girl could see through the thicket of trees, making out some yellow lights.

Marsha was inert and as immobile as a mountain. She mumbled something incoherent, her chin settling on her chest, and she slipped further down toward unconsciousness, edging toward a coma.

The little girl turned and tottered away, making for the welcoming lights of Michael McCann's house.

Since the theft of his beloved fortune, Michael McCann had redoubled his passion for his work. He hardly slept anymore, working from dawn until deep into the night. The three doses of vodka were a thing of the past. Nothing, not even belts of harsh, cheap liquor could eradicate the pain, so he forced himself to live with it, driving himself to work harder than he had ever worked before.

The pieces of furniture he designed and built were becoming more elaborate, more finely made, as though the only care he could bother to take was with the inanimate objects. Even with his intensified work schedule, it was taking longer and longer for Michael to complete a piece of furniture. His meticulous concern for detail overwhelmed his timetable.

Commissions were late in being delivered, but few customers complained. Most were aware that they were getting exceptional objects, yet paying only a fraction of their true worth. Michael knew he was cheating himself, but it didn't matter to him. He just didn't care any longer.

Michael was working late that night, of course, completely unaware of the passage of time. He was toiling at his bench, painstakingly sanding by hand a small piece of wood, an interior strut for a table top, a minute bit of a much larger whole that no one would ever see or care about. But it was important to Michael that it be perfect. His mind was blank, focused completely on the task at hand.

So concentrated with his mind, that it took him a few moments to figure out the source of the piercing shriek that suddenly filled his little house. Michael's head snapped around and glared at the kettle whistling on the stove top. He could scarcely remember putting it on and could only wonder how long it had been whistling before he had noticed it.

Michael forced himself away from his workbench, stretching stiffly as he made his way into the kitchen. He shivered and realized that he was cold. The fire in the grate, a roaring blaze a few hours earlier, had now dwindled down to nothing. There were no logs in the wood bin next to the fireplace, and he did not feel like venturing out into the cold night for more. He made a cup of tea and sipped it, toying with the idea of going to bed, but deciding against it. A few more hours work and he would go to sleep the instant his head touched the pillow; if he went to bed now, he would be tortured with fifteen or twenty minutes of dark wakefulness. He could certainly do without a quarter of an hour of brooding.

Michael dug an old electric heater out of a closet and plugged the fraying wire into a socket. The instant he flipped the switch to turn it on, there was a spark and an electrical crack. A fuse blew out and the entire house was suffused in darkness.

"Goddammit!"

Michael blundered about in the gloom for a moment or two, feeling his way around and navigating by the waning orange glow of the fire. He found a flashlight in the jumble of junk in the kitchen drawer and snapped it on. It seemed that he would be going out into the cold after all—the fuse box and fuses were in the musty cellar beneath his house and the entrance was outside.

Cursing under his breath, Michael trudged out into the snow, the feeble beam of the old flashlight hardly denting the black of the night. He missed completely the little girl standing knee deep in the snow just a few feet from his front door. By the time he had made his way into the cellar, grappled with the antique fuse box for a few unpleasant minutes, got his lights on again, and returned to the cabin, she had vanished.

The hell with the cold, Michael McCann decided. He found his mug of tea and drank it in a gulp or two, absorbing the warmth. Then he returned to his workbench. He settled there and picked up his sanding block, turning his attention to the small piece of wood clamped in the vise. As he examined it, his shoulders slumped and he rubbed his eyes. The intense, mesmerizing spell of his work had been shattered by the interruption. There was nothing he could do but go to bed and hope that he could fight off his night demons until sleep claimed him.

Michael snapped off the light on the workbench and stumbled toward his bed, not bothering to undress, merely kicking off his heavy boots. Like felled tree, he toppled onto the bed and lay still, an arm thrown heavily over his eyes, as if blocking out the night itself.

Then he became aware that he was not alone in the bed.

Michael shrieked, jumped out of the bed, and snapped on the light on the night table.

Marsha's little girl was curled in the bed, her big blue eyes fixed on him. His jaw dropped—it seemed like it dropped almost to the floor and his eyes grew as wide as a pair of Liberty gold-dollar pieces. The effect was extravagantly comic and the little girl giggled as if he was a professional clown going through his funniest of slapstick routines.

"Good grief," he whispered, "where the hell did you spring from?"

The child scrambled out of bed and walked toward him. Michael, for his part, backed away as though she were a rabid dog or an intruder hell-bent on murder. He lunged toward the fireplace and grabbed the heavy brass-handled poker, waving it menacingly. The child stopped in her tracks and the smile vanished from her face. He looked at the girl, then at the blunt instrument he was brandishing, and realized that the poker was a bit of overkill. The little girl was scarcely more than a toddler. Michael figured he could keep her under control without having to beat her to jelly with a poker that probably weighed more than she did.

The little girl took hold of the seam of his pants and tugged on it. "Mommy?" she said softly, her little voice full of hope.

"Mommy?" he repeated, as if the word were foreign to him. "Mommy? Boy, are you off. Mommy . . . My God. No, I'm not your mommy."

"Mommy?" the child repeated, as if he hadn't quite gotten it the first time.

"No," he snapped. "Wait . . . Mommy? Where is your mommy? Do you know where your mommy is?"

The little girl said nothing.

Then he noticed that her clothes were wet and that there was moisture in her hair. Her mommy must be close by, outside, trapped, perhaps, in the snowstorm. He bolted toward the door then stopped. The little intruder was right behind him, intending, it seemed, to follow him out into the night.

"Stop!" he ordered. Obediently, the girl stopped. In her short life, she had learned from experience with Dwayne that an angry adult voice was meant to be obeyed. The consequences could be very nasty. "Stay! Sit! Sit."

The girl sat and watched uncomprehending as he dashed out the front door.

It didn't take him long to find Marsha. He followed the faint imprint of the child's footsteps in the snow and they led him directly to a snow-dusted bundle slung under the low branches of a pine tree.

Michael threw himself to his knees in front of her and brushed back the snow, grasping her wrist to search for a pulse. Marsha's skin was deathly cold, but damp, as if the light of life within her had only recently been extinguished. Her half-closed eyes were blank and unseeing. He had never actually encountered a corpse before, but he realized that he did not need a degree in medicine to realize that this thin, bedraggled woman was dead.

Michael jumped back from the body, horror-stricken at his discovery. "Oh, my God . . ." Then he turned and raced back into the house.

The little girl was sitting perfectly still and had not strayed an inch from where he left her.

"Mommy?" she said.

"Uh . . . no . . . we . . . we have to go find your mommy. Right now." He dragged a coarse, scratchy army blanket from the bed and wrapped his tiny visitor in it. Michael picked her up—she weighed practically nothing—and dashed outside to his truck and drove off, making for town.

As the old pickup rattled along, Michael kept glancing to his right, peeking at the little girl, as if still not quite able to believe that she was there. Never before, not when he had been drinking, not even when his money had been stolen, had he been as surprised as he was then.

As they raced by Newland's property, Michael suddenly stood on the brakes, the old truck skidding to a halt on the slick road. At the head of the driveway was a parked police cruiser.

"Police," said Michael. "That's what I want." He steered the car up the driveway and gunned the old engine, charging up to the front door of the mansion.

Although many of the guests had departed, the party was still going strong. The house was ablaze with lights, and music filtered out into the night air. When the front door swung open, none of the revelers noticed at first. But then one, then another stopped midsentence and stared. Framed in the doorway, the little girl in his arms, stood Michael McCann, snow in his hair, a wild, almost mad look in his eyes.

"Does anyone know this child?"

The party came to an abrupt halt. For a moment, no one could speak. The scene was just too amazing to take in all at once. Here was Burrows's least-known citizen appearing in the house of the town's best known—with a strange, emaciated child in his arms. April Simon noted the sudden silence and came running. When she saw the scene, all she could say was: "My God . . ."

It was Cal Mosely who recovered first. "What the hell is this all about, McCann?"

Michael ignored him. "I want the doctor," he said. "The doctor is here, isn't he?" As he spoke, the blanket draped around the little girl came loose and fell away, revealing her face and her heart-covered pajamas. John Newland recognized them instantly. He did his best to keep his composure, but inside his chest, his heart was hammering. If this was his little girl then Marsha Swanson couldn't be far behind. If she suddenly appeared here and started shooting off her mouth . . . John Newland's stomach lurched.

"Let's not ruin the party," he said, hoping his voice sounded commanding. "Put her in a bedroom and we'll get Dr. Roberts."

Michael shook his head. "It's not for her. There's a woman lying in the snow outside my house."

John Newland paled. "A woman? What woman?"

"I don't know," said Michael. "I think she's dead."

"Oh, no," said April Simon.

Michael McCann's words had a different effect on John Newland. He relaxed a little bit. Maybe things would turn out for the best after all.

As if on cue, everybody sprang into action. "Someone get the doctor," John Newland ordered. "Mrs. Simon, take the child. We have to get out to the McCann house right away."

"Yes, Mr. Newland."

"I'll radio the station," said one of the cops.

April Simon reached for the child, but the instant she left Michael's arms, she started to scream, loud impassioned wails full of anguish and misery.

"It's okay, honey," April said soothingly. "It's all right. Everything's going to be just fine." The child choked on her cries, filled her tiny lungs with air, and again let out a long, forlorn cry. Michael couldn't stand it. He took the child back, and almost immediately she stopped crying. The little girl clung to him, sniffing and staring at his face, as if beseeching him not to let her go.

"Don't worry," he said. "Don't worry. Mrs. Simon is nice and kind. You'll be safe with her. She's a good person." Gingerly, as if afraid of unsettling a delicate mechanism, Michael passed the little girl back to April.

"It's okay," Mrs. Simon said. "You'll stay with me tonight, baby, you'll stay with me."

"McCann," said Newland, "take us to the spot. Show us where you found the woman."

Michael nodded and began to walk toward the door. John Newland quickly whispered in Nancy Lammeter's ear. "Will you wait here?" he asked.

"Why would I leave?" she said simply.

It required nothing more than a little police paperwork to bring Marsha Swanson's brief unhappy life to an official end. Dr. Roberts examined the corpse with some care and listed the official cause of death as hypothermia.

"But it could have been anything," he told John Newland and Michael McCann. "She was a heavy heroin user. Her heart just gave up." He filled out the death certificate, resting the official form on the hood of a police cruiser. "Shame about the kid, too. Damaged goods."

"Damaged goods?" said Michael. "What do you mean?"

"The children of addicts have a whole raft of medical problems. Brain damage, motor neuron disorders, infections." His pen was poised over the space for name of the deceased. "Any idea who she was?"

John Newland shook his head. "*I've* never seen her before," he said quickly.

"Never said you did, John," Dr. Roberts responded mildly. "I guess I was just thinking out loud. I'll just put her down as a Jane Doe."

"I guess that would be best," said Newland. It was all he could do to suppress a smile. His heart felt light. Marsha Swanson was dead and he was finally free. As to the little girl at that moment sleeping peacefully at April Simon's warm house, he gave no thought at all.

But John Newland thought nothing of "his" little girl, Michael McCann could not think of anything else.

Once the police and the ambulance bearing the corpse of Marsha Swanson had left the property and silence had once again descended on the tumbledown little house, Michael had changed into his pajamas and gone to bed. But sleep would not come. He tossed and turned for an hour, unable to find comfort in his own bed. Everytime he closed his eyes, he saw that frail child, he heard her giggles, and her anguished scream when she had been taken from his arms. He could still feel the tiny weight of her in his arms, as if her body had left its impression on his hands like a burn.

He heard Dr. Roberts's voice, flat and dispassionate, dismiss her as damaged goods. . . .

Michael swept away the tangled sheets and sat

up in bed and put his head in his hands. If the little girl was damaged goods, then so was he. Between the dour carpenter and the bewildered child there existed a common bond, a shared experience that easily bridged the vast gulf of age and history. They were both orphaned by the unfairness of life, betrayed by the very people they had every reason to trust.

Michael McCann got out of bed, pulled on his boots, and threw on his old parka over his pajamas, and got into his truck. A few minutes later he was knocking on the door of April Simon's house. She did not seem at all surprised to see him, welcoming him with few words, but with a warm smile that spoke volumes.

"She's in the back bedroom" she said. "I'll make some coffee."

"Thank you," Michael mumbled. For a moment he was embarrassed, flustered that his emotions, so carefully concealed for so long, were now so obvious.

The little girl was curled in a cradle, sleeping soundly. Michael gazed at her, ruffled her silken hair, and allowed himself a smile.

"You're not damaged goods," he whispered, "are you?"

9

Michael awoke with a start, slumped in an armchair in a room filled with light. Rubbing his eyes, he tried to recall where he was, what had happened. Then he looked into the crib next to him and remembered. The little girl was standing up, holding on to the railing of the baby bed, staring fixedly at him, as if willing him awake with her blue eyes.

"Hi," he said and was rewarded with a smile.

April Simon bustled into the room. "Sleep well?" she asked.

"Yeah. Great." Michael stood up and stretched. A few hours of sleep scrunched in an armchair in a strange house had not been particularly comfortable, but he didn't care.

"Okay, honey," said Mrs. Simon. She reached into the crib and picked up the child and laid her on the small single bed in the corner of the room. "Let's get this show on the road."

"What are you going to do?" Michael asked.

"I'm going to change her diaper," she said. "She's probably wet *and* filthy."

"Diaper?" he said, greatly alarmed. "I

think . . . I better . . ." He pointed toward the door. "Listen, I'll just wait outside, okay?"

April Simon shrugged. "Suit yourself. But if you stay, you might learn a thing or two." It was a thrown gauntlet, a direct challenge to prove his courage. Michael realized that he had no alternative but to accept the dare or lessen himself in Mrs. Simon's eyes. He still had enough ego left to not want to look like a coward.

"Okay," he said, trying to sound nonchalant. "Sure."

Briskly, with the capable hands of a mother, April Simon extracted the little girl from her tattered pajamas and stripped open the tapes that secured her disposable diaper.

Michael forced himself to look. "Wooh! What *is* that?"

"Well . . ."—Mrs. Simon reached for a handful of baby wipes and went to work cleaning up—"it goes by a number of names. Poop. Poopy. Pooh. Pooh-pooh. But I believe that the scientific term is doo-doo."

"Oh. Doo-doo," he said, as if committing an unfamiliar word to memory. "Got it."

"There you go, honey," said April Simon. "All nice and clean now."

The little girl smiled and giggled as Mrs. Simon held her by the ankles, raised her legs and skillfully placed a fresh diaper under her. With a deftness that made a complicated process seem ridiculously easy, she diapered the child, pressed down the tapes and stood her up. "All done!"

"Whew." Michael sighed, relieved, as if Mrs.

Simon had just completed a triple bypass. "Now what?"

"I'm going to dress her. I've got some of my son's old clothes here. Let's see what fits . . ."

Under Mrs. Simon's expert hands, it took no time at all to dress the little girl in a bodysuit called a onesy, a yellow T-shirt, and a pair of faded denim trousers.

"Now," said April, "we are faced with the task of seeing how much food we can transfer from the jar of baby food and into the baby."

"Feeding. We're going to feed the kid," said Michael.

"A deceptively simple term," said April Simon, mysteriously. "Come on, honey."

She settled the little girl in a high chair in the kitchen and tied a bib under her chin.

"Step one," said April. "The big buildup."

"The big buildup," Michael repeated dutifully.

She took a small jar of orange baby food from the pantry. "What's this?" Mrs. Simon's voice was filled with exaggerated wonderment and awe. "Mixed garden vegetables! Mmmmmmmmm-*mmm*. Does that sound yummy or what? What's in this?" She studied the label intently. "Oh, my goodness! Peas! Squash! Beets! Green beans!" She shook her head, amazed that something so delicious could be contained in such a small jar. "Did you ever hear of anything so delicious in your whole life?"

Michael heard his cue, but he messed it up. "Well . . . uh . . . I guess not."

The little girl was staring at April, her mouth

open and her eyes wide, plainly amazed by the performance that was taking place.

April Simon popped the lid, dabbed the spoon into the ocher mush, and tasted a microscopic dab. "Oh, wow!" She rolled her eyes and seemed to go into ecstasy, like a gourmet dining in a fine, five-star restaurant.

"This is soooooo delicious! Yummy-yum-yummmmmmm." Then she got a sly look on her face. "Would you like some? Would you like to try a little bit of this wonderful, yummy stuff?"

The little girl nodded eagerly and raised her little hands, as if ready to seize the glass container and drink it down in a single gulp. But Mrs. Simon held the jar close to her chest, as if unwilling to let it go.

"Nope," she said with a shake of her head. "I think I'll keep it. All for me."

The little girl whimpered and waved her hands. "Nooooo," she cried.

"You want some? You really, really want some?"

The little girl nodded vigorously.

Mrs. Simon loaded up the spoon with a healthy dollop of the orange paste. "Lemme see how wide you can open your mouth. Wide. Wide. Wider . . ." Then, with the precision of a surgeon, she deposited the food on the little girl's tongue. Her mouth closed, she swallowed. A look of intense disappointment crossed her little features.

"Now comes the hard part," said Mrs. Simon.

It took a little longer to ease the next spoonful into the girl. She turned her head and squirmed in the seat, bobbing and weaving like a very small boxer, trying to avoid the relentless spoon. Every few minutes, though, she surrendered to the inevitable and opened her mouth.

"There you go. Goooood girl. See, it's not so bad, is it? Come on. One more spoonful. One more . . . there you go. . . ." She turned to Michael. "Want to try?"

"You said one more and she had one more."

"I lied."

Michael took the spoon and the jar of baby food, loaded up, aimed and scored a success the first time out placing the food on the little tongue without mishap.

"Beginner's luck," said April.

And she was right. The second spoonful he deposited in the little girl's nostril. The next somehow found its way into her golden hair. By the time the jar was empty much of the mixed garden vegetables had been smeared on the little girl's face, but the greater part had gotten inside her.

Michael was exhausted. "Now what?"

"She has a doctor's appointment."

"You made a doctor's appointment for her?"

April Simon shook her head. "I didn't. The county did. She's officially a ward of the state, remember?"

"Ward of the state." Michael McCann's heart sank. The words had a curiously cold, archaic implication to them. "Ward of the state" sounded to him like something from a Victorian novel—some sad story of widows and orphans living in abject poverty, striving to avoid the hell of the workhouse. He could see no relation between that callous official term and this sunny little girl.

"Let's go," said April.

April and Michael sat in the background of the examining room at the Burrows clinic, watching as Dr. Roberts meticulously examined his little patient. He shone lights in her eyes and tapped her knees, felt her lymph nodes, and poked and probed and listened to her little heart.

After a while he said: "Hmmmmmmm," in that doctorish sort of way that could mean that you only had six months to live or were in better shape than an Olympic decathlete.

Always fearing the worst, Michael almost jumped when he heard that noncommittal sound. "Hmmmm? What does that mean? What is it? What's wrong?"

"Nothing," said Dr. Roberts, pulling the earpieces of his stethoscope from his ears. "Absolutely nothing."

Michael allowed himself to resume breathing.

"There's no sign of addiction or even past addiction. Strange. No FAS either."

"FAS?" asked April Simon.

"Fetal alcohol syndrome," said the doctor. "The mother may have been an addict, but it seems that she was responsible enough not to do drugs or drink during pregnancy. Or . . . "

"Or?"

"Or it could have been one of those things. Luck of the draw."

The little girl sensed that the examination was over. She toddled over to Michael and clutched at his pants leg, beseeching him to pick her up.

"She likes you the most," said April. "She wants to sit on your lap."

"Oh. Okay." He hoisted her up and she settled on his knees, content.

"We should get her over to the county orphanage in Elderfield right away. The sooner the county starts the process, the better off she'll be."

"The process?" Like "ward of the state" this term seemed unfeelingly bureaucratic and remote from the child herself. "The process of what exactly?"

"The process of adoption, of course."

"Adoption?" said Michael, alarmed.

"Well, just what did you think was going to happen to her? They'll take her to Elderfield for processing, and then they'll release her into temporary foster care. Then, somewhere down the road, someone will adopt her. At least, that's what we should all hope for. The more disruption a child undergoes at this stage, the worse it is for her later on."

"I could do it," said Mrs. Simon. "I don't mind being foster mother for a while. It would be cutting out the middle man. No orphanage. One less disruption . . ."

"But where will she end up ultimately?" asked

Michael. It was beginning to dawn on him that he might never see this child again.

Dr. Roberts shrugged and shook his head. "No way to tell. One thing you can be sure of, she won't be adopted around here. There's a big demand for adoptable children in California. If I were to guess, I would say she's headed west."

"She's alone," said Michael gravely. "And I'm alone."

"Huh?" said Mrs. Simon.

"What do you mean?"

Like a diver poised on the edge of a high board, Michael McCann drew a deep breath, then took the plunge. "She came to replace my money, you know. It was no accident that she came to my house. . . . What if I kept her?"

"You?" Dr. Roberts could hardly believe his ears. "McCann, what the hell do *you* know about babies?"

"I can feed 'em, I can diaper 'em," said Michael proudly. "And I know at least four synonyms for excrement."

Dr. Roberts fixed a long, hard look on Michael McCann, as if toying with the idea of committing him to the county insane asylum which, by coincidence, was also in Elderfield. Then he seemed to think the better of it. He shook his head slowly, amazed at what he was about to do.

"Mrs. Simon, you'd be prepared to take care of the little girl during the adoption procedure?"

"Of course," she said forcefully.

"You know, Mr. McCann, that the state will do a thorough investigation into you, your fitness to be a father. Any skeletons in your closet and they'll find them.'' He paused a moment and then added: ''That's the theory, anyway.''

''I have nothing to hide,'' said Michael. But he wondered if being dead for the better part of the last five years would count against him.

The Virginia Department of Child Welfare moved no faster than any other state agency, but John Newland intervened on behalf of Michael's petition, moving his adoption application to the head of the list. No one in the little town would have thought Newland's interest in the case anything out of the ordinary, had they known about it—after all, Michael McCann was a constituent, and presumably, a voter. For his part, John Newland wasn't sure why he was using his clout to advance McCann's cause. More than likely he thought that the faster the little girl was adopted and off the books, the sooner any unpleasant details about her birth and background might emerge.

Any discomfort John Newland may have felt about having the girl so close to home was lessened by the thought that here in Virginia he would be able to control or hush up any problems that might arise. The adoption processes in other states might have been more thorough than here, and they would have been more or less beyond his authority.

Michael McCann faced the approaching interview with the Child Welfare authorities with mounting apprehension. The meeting was to take place in his home so that the investigators could judge the quality of life the adoptee was likely to enjoy. The adoption guidelines were straightforward: The child could only be placed in a safe, secure, stable, loving household. Financial considerations of the prospective parents were taken into account, but were not paramount.

"Safe, secure, stable, loving." Michael must have spoken those words a thousand times in the weeks before the interview. He had examined every inch of his house during that time, making it safe. All of his tools were locked up and beyond the reach of prying little hands. He had rewired the fuse box to make sure that there would never again be electrical problems. Security was improved too—there was a new dead bolt on the front door, and shiny brass latches on every window. The only hazard in the immediate vicinity that he could see was the old water-filled quarry that stood at the farthest reach of the Newland property. Michael wondered if he could be held responsible for geographical features. In his lighter, hopeful moments he doubted that he could be. But who knew what unreasonable actions a state agency was capable of . . .?

The requirements of stability and affection he knew he had in spades. All it would take would be to convince the examiners that he had them. In all honesty, he had misgivings about his ability to translate his inchoate, but intensely felt feelings into words.

The house had been scrubbed clean—there was not a speck of dust or a cobweb anywhere, and the wooden floors had been buffed until they shone. There was not an object out of place—Michael didn't know if the inspectors were allowed complete access to the entire house, but assuming that they were, every cupboard and every drawer had been organized. If he was not going to get custody, it would not be because he had packed teaspoons with tablespoons in the kitchen drawers or stacked towels with the sheets in the linen closet.

April Simon looked over Michael and his house on the morning of the interview. She was impressed with the perfect cleaning job.

"You've missed your calling," she said. "You could be a world-class cleaning lady."

"Does everything look all right?"

"Beautiful."

"And do *I* look all right?" Michael could not remember the last time he had worn a jacket, tie, and a pair of trousers that required the services of an iron. The clothes smelled faintly of mothballs, and were more redolent his long-ago life in a distant, dead world.

April straightened his tie. "You look very nice," she said. She smoothed the shoulders of the old tweed jacket. "Just remember to be yourself. That's all it takes. Just be yourself and you'll see everything will turn out for the best. That's what they say, anyway."

Michael felt a bolt of panic shoot through him. "Myself? Myself! I don't have a self."

She patted his cheek. "Sure you do. Relax, and it will come out. You'll see."

But Michael was far from relaxed when the two social workers, a man and a woman, arrived at his front door. He showed them into the house, fighting the wildly divergent urges flooding through him. One second he was inclined to jabber like an idiot, peppering them with questions without waiting for a reply—"How do you do? Nice to meet you. Have any trouble finding the place? My, what a nice dress. Pretty day, isn't it?"

He took in their bewildered looks and immediately fell prey to his other urge, lapsing into a stony, impenetrable silence. Michael was sweating under his jacket, well aware that he had not gotten off to a good start.

With great difficulty, he took command of himself and ushered his guests into the kitchen, seated them at the table there, and determined that they did not want coffee, tea, or a glass of water.

The female social worker was named Ms. Andrews; her colleague Mr. Hopkins. They did not offer first names. They both had clipboards, which they carried like badges of office, and government-issue ballpoint pens, which they clicked officiously.

Ms. Andrews led off. "Now then, Mr. uh . . ." She consulted her clipboard. "Mr. McCann. Tell us about yourself." They both smiled smiles which Michael imagined were also official government issue.

It was, of course, precisely the sort of question

that is calculated to make any nervous would-be parent even more nervous and tongue-tied.

"Me? I . . . Well. Let me see. I'm . . . I don't understand the question." He smiled diffidently, but his face fell when the two social workers exchanged quick, disapproving looks.

"You live alone?" asked Mr. Hopkins.

Finally, a question he could answer. Michael nodded vigorously. "Yes. Alone. Absolutely alone. I'm divorced, you see. No one here but me."

Ms. Andrews and Mr. Hopkins frowned, and they both made minute and identical marks on the papers on their clipboards.

"Tell us, do you think you'd make a good father?" asked Ms. Andrews.

The answer should have been obvious—who, afterall, having applied to adopt a child would reply: "Well, now that you mention it, I don't think I'd make a particularly good father. Sorry to have wasted your time." But Michael pondered this question and his answer before replying.

"Yes," he said finally. "Yes, I do believe I would make a good father."

"Uh-huh," said Ms. Andrews, as though he hadn't quite succeeded in erasing her skepticism. They both made two more tiny marks on their papers.

"Do you own any property?" asked Mr. Hopkins.

"Property?" Michael asked, as though he had never heard the word before.

"This house, for example?" said Ms. Andrews, as though throwing a drowning man a life preserver. "Do you own this house?"

"Ah, no. I rent this from Mr. Newland."

Two more disapproving looks were exchanged and two more microscopic entries went into his file.

Mr. Hopkins decided to pursue this line of questioning. "You own no substantial property at all?" His tone of voice suggested a hard-charging district attorney hammering away at a hostile witness.

Michael was getting flustered. He hated himself for it, but he was beginning to stammer and stutter like a dimwit. "Property? Well . . . uh, I *did* have some property. Quite a lot of it. Valuable, I mean. But . . . but I had it stolen."

He paused a moment, as if analyzing his own words and decided, disastrously, that they needed some clarifying. "I mean, it was stolen from me. If I *had* it stolen it sounds like I asked someone to steal it, which I didn't. Really. I had it taken. By a thief or, you see, not a thief exactly, but a thiefly sort of person."

He knew he had to wrestle his sentences back on track, but he failed. Instead they just petered out. "It was mine and stolen by . . . I mean . . . you know . . . don't you?"

"You were robbed?" said Mr. Hopkins.

"That is correct," said Michael miserably. The two social workers did not even bother with even a minuscule mark this time. Former ownership of valuable property counted for nothing with the Department of Child Welfare.

"Have you ever spent much time around children?" Ms. Andrews asked.

"No." Then: "Yes."

Mr. Hopkins pursed his lips. "Is that a yes? Or is that a no?"

"It's a yes. A definite yes! I used to be a schoolteacher. It's almost impossible to avoid spending time around children if that happens to be your profession, wouldn't it?" He was delighted that he had dredged up his old occupation. It was so far back in his past, so deeply buried in his memory, that it had almost completely slipped his mind. *Score one for me*, he thought.

But his two interrogators managed to turn even this innocent answer against him. "*Used* to be?" said Ms. Andrews forcefully. "Am I to understand that teaching school is no longer your profession?"

"Uh, yes."

"And while teaching, you actively sought to *avoid* the children under your care?"

Michael shook his head. "No, of course not."

"But you said—"

Michael couldn't help cutting her off and his voice was a little louder than he meant it to be. "What I *said* was that even if you wanted to avoid children, you couldn't if you were a teacher. As it happened, I did not want to avoid them. I just said it would be impossible to do. That's all."

"Temper, temper, temper," said Mr. Hopkins with an evil little smile.

"I'm sorry," said Michael. "I should answer these questions honestly, shouldn't I?"

"Of course," said Ms. Andrews. "If you are not going to answer honestly, then there is little point in continuing this interview, is there?"

"No. Honesty was always my intention," Michael mumbled. "Sorry about that."

Mr. Hopkins wasn't making minute marks on his chart now, he was writing furiously. Without looking up, he fired off his next question. "Have you ever had children of your own?"

"Yes . . . uh, no."

Both social workers stared at him. "Which is it this time?" asked Ms. Andrews.

"No." He was staring at the floor, as if entertaining a faint hope that the old boards might suddenly open up and swallow him whole.

"Are you a homosexual?"

Now he looked up sharply. "No! No, not that I know of. . . . I mean I'm not. That is, I have never noticed any interest in that area. I am completely not homosexual."

"I am," said Mr. Hopkins.

"Oh," said Michael, aghast at his gaff. "Congratulations."

Ms. Andrews consulted her papers. "How could you, a single man, take care of this child?"

"Well," he said, "this is how I would do it. I would wake in the morning, take care of the child and then, when she went to sleep, I would go to sleep."

Ms. Andrews pounced with what she thought would be the knockout blow. "What about when you have to go to work? What would you do then?''

''I wouldn't go to work,'' said Michael earnestly. ''I mean, I work at home. I wouldn't have to leave. Ever.''

''And what work do you do, Mr. McCann?'' asked Mr. Hopkins.

''I make furniture. In fact, I could offer you both a nice armoire if . . .'' Michael smiled a sickly smile. ''Uh, forget it.''

''It's not that easy to raise a child,'' said Ms. Andrews sternly.

Michael nodded. ''I am aware of that, but nothing is easy.'' He breathed deeply. ''Look, could I talk to you plainly, man to man?''

''Man to man?'' said Ms. Andrews.

''I mean, man to woman to man to man, uh, homosexual man.'' He wiped the sweat from his brow. ''I mean, all I'm trying to say is that I'm not very good at interviews. . . .''

''No,'' said Ms. Andrews, ''they do not appear to be your strong suit.''

''I know that . . . so I am asking you to overlook everything that you've heard so far, forget what you see. I mean, it's sort of like''—he looked up as if the rafters of the house would provide him with a suitable metaphor for his predicament—''it's sort of like Jell-O.''

''Jell-O?'' said Mr. Hopkins.

''Yes, yes,'' said Michael warming to the image. ''See, Jell-O might not look all that appetizing, all quivery in a bowl in front of you, but it actually, when you try it, the stuff turns out to taste quite good."

"Jell-O?" said Ms. Andrews, as if it was her turn to say the word.

"See, it doesn't look good, but it tastes good. I don't look good to you right now, but I know that I could take care of that little girl. If you gave her to me, you could stop by in a year or so, and I'm sure that you would be impressed by what you'd see."

The two social workers looked at him with rather severe expressions on their faces.

Michael's heart sank and he played his last card. "I believe that this child belongs to me," he said solemnly. "She walked into my house."

In their years of social work, Ms. Andrews and Mr. Hopkins had heard hundreds and hundreds of reasons for permitting adoptions, but this was the first time they had been asked to sanction an adoption under the age-old rule of finders-keepers.

"We'll be in touch, Mr. McCann," said Ms. Andrews. At least, those were the words she actually uttered. What she really meant was: Don't get your hopes up.

Neither of the social workers had the slightest misgivings about not recommending Michael McCann as an adoptive father. It wasn't that he was a bad man, or a menace to society. It was more that he was an eccentric, a flake who had lived so long in a narrow landscape of his own making, he had more or less forgotten how to function in the real world. Ms. Andrews and Mr. Hopkins spelled this out in the correct bureaucratic language, filed their reports with their superiors, and moved on to the next case. In the normal course of business it would take only a matter of weeks until the unconventional Michael McCann would be nothing more than a dim memory. In a month, they would have forgotten him completely.

But in their brief interview, Ms. Andrews and Mr. Hopkins had failed to realize a single truth: that where Michael McCann was concerned, nothing proceeded normally. Not twenty-four hours after they had filed their negative report on Michael, the folder was returned to them, along with a note from their boss, the commissioner herself, suggesting that they might have been a bit hasty in so quickly rejecting Michael McCann as a candidate.

Both of the social workers knew what this meant. It was plain that Mr. McCann had some powerful friends somewhere up the line, and that pressure had been applied or future favors promised. Dutifully, Andrews and Hopkins rewrote their report to suggest that Michael McCann would be an excellent parent and that custody of the little girl should be granted without prejudice and without delay. . . .

Michael was at home, painstakingly turning a table leg on a hand-operated lathe when there came a knock at his door. He was expecting no one, of course, and he almost fainted when he opened his front door to find Hopkins, Andrews, and Dr. Roberts gathered there. Mr. Hopkins held the baby in his arms.

"Congratulations, Mr. McCann," said Mr. Hopkins, presenting the baby to him, as if he had won a trophy.

To say that Michael was stunned would be something of an understatement. He took the little girl in his arms, holding her tenderly, gingerly, as if afraid that she would break in his strong callused hands.

"I don't believe it. . . . This really can't be happening, can it?"

"Believe it, McCann," said Dr. Roberts, gruffly. At John Newland's behest, he had given his guarantee to the commissioner of the child welfare agency that this little girl would be well taken care of.

Ms. Andrews still had her doubts about the whole undertaking, and she did not bother to hide her disapproval. "There is some paperwork we have to attend to," she said, her voice clipped and dry.

"Of course."

They sat at the kitchen table while Michael signed a dozen different documents. He didn't bother to read them, knowing as he did that nothing they stated could have given him pause—all he knew was that these documents were all that stood between him and fatherhood. As he signed, Dr. Roberts filled him in on a few unofficial details of the adoption, Michael listening with one ear only. He kept on sneaking peeks at his new little girl, his heart expanding with pride until he thought his chest would not be able to contain it.

The last bit of paper signed attested to the fact that he had received the child in good condition. The Department of Child Welfare even supplied him with a starter kit of formula, some baby bottles, and a package of diapers.

In a matter of minutes, Michael was alone with his new daughter. In spite of all they had gone through together, and the fact that he had never wavered in his desire to adopt this little girl, now that they were alone, father and child were shy and awkward with each other. Michael wasn't quite sure what to do next, when his gaze fell on the little packet of supplies that the social workers had left behind.

"Hey!" he said, delighted that he had something to do. "I'll bet you're really, really hungry."

The little girl nodded. " 'Ungry."

"Then let's see what we have here. . . ." He rummaged in the parcel and extracted a large, thirty-two ounce can of high-iron baby formula. He remembered April Simon's instructions: Give the food a big build up.

"This looks pretty good," he said, his voice dripping with cunning. "Wanna try it out?"

The little girl nodded again. "Uh-huh."

"Wellll . . . we'll see about that." The instructions said that the formula was best served warm.

"Okay," he said. "No problem." He opened the can and poured some into a saucepan on top of the stove. While the liquid heated, he prepared the bottle and the nipple, pretty sure he was doing everything correctly. What, he wondered, was all the fuss about? This child-rearing business appeared to be a piece of cake.

"Well, hello, Mama!"

Michael turned to see April Simon standing in the doorway, smiling from ear to ear. She carried a stuffed duffel bag in her arms, and at her side was her little boy, a three-year-old named Lawrence.

"Have you considered growing some breasts?" she asked.

"Don't have to," said Michael. "I have high-iron infant formula. A gift of the state of Virginia."

"They think of everything, don't they." She walked into the house and hugged the little girl. "Hi, honey. How does it feel to be home at last?"

The child smiled and shyly took cover behind Michael's leg, peeking out from time to time, as if she had never seen April Simon before in her life.

"You know," said April. "I never wanted you to get your hopes up. I thought a single man getting a baby has about the same odds as me getting a single man."

"Miracles can happen. . . . I asked Dr. Roberts how this one happened and he said, 'Don't ask,' so I'm not. I think I'm a quasi-foster parent, with a twist of an arm and a favor outside the system."

April laughed. "Well, finally, corruption on behalf of the good guys. I brought a whole bag of baby stuff. Things that Lawrence grew out of years ago."

"Thanks." Michael bustled about, as if anxious to prove to his audience that he was already an old hand in the baby business. He took the pot of formula off the stove, poured the liquid into the bottle and screwed down the ring and the nipple.

"Can I cook or can I cook?" He held the bottle out for inspection as if it was a dish of beef Wellington or some other tricky gourmet dish.

"You better tap some on your wrist before you give it to her," April Simon cautioned.

"Tap some on my wrist? Why?" He squirted a little of the formula on to the back of his hand. "Yeow!" The formula was scalding hot.

"That's why," said April.

"What do I do?"

"Cool it down, stupid. Run the bottle under cold water until it's cool enough to drink."

"Good idea."

"Did they find out anything?" she asked. "About the mother or the father?"

Michael nodded. "They tracked the mother's car to an address in Cabbagetown, down in Norfolk. The neighbors said that there was a man living there, but they said he vanished."

"Lucky break for you. . . . You're going to have to give her a name, you know." They both looked down at the little girl. She had forsaken her hiding place behind Michael's leg and had ventured over to Lawrence. The two of them were rolling on the floor, giggling and wrestling.

"A name? Yeah. I have been thinking about that. It's not easy, you know."

"Yeah, but you must have some thoughts on the subject. Right?"

Michael nodded. In fact, he had a name all picked out—it had been ready for years now. "I'd like to call her Mathilda."

April Simon paled. "I will give you the deed of my house if you don't call her Mathilda."

"Why? It's a lovely name."

"Oh, absolutely," she said sarcastically. "Except that she'll spend her whole life spelling it out to credit card companies and clerks at the Department of Motor Vehicles. And people will shorten it to something like 'Tildy.' Ugh."

"I realize all that. But that's what I've decided to call her." Then as if trying it out, he picked up the little girl and held her high over his head. "Hi, Mathilda!"

Mathilda laughed and squirmed in his arms. "Hi."

"See? She likes it."

April Simon still had her doubts. "Okay," she said slowly. "Just promise me one thing . . ."

"Anything."

"If anyone calls her 'Tildy,' you have to kill them."

Michael grinned. "Deal."

10

Over the years, Michael McCann had provided quite a bit of entertainment to the citizens of Burrows, Virginia, without being aware that he was doing so. However, nothing he had done to date had been half so diverting as adopting the little girl who was now known as Mathilda McCann. The first time he appeared in town pushing his daughter in a stroller—well, it was if a circus parade had suddenly appeared on Main Street.

Dad, the chief of police, was the first to spot father and daughter. He gaped and craned his neck, almost driving his cruiser through the front door of town hall. The crowd at the Rainbow Bar filled the plate-glass window, all of them pushing and shoving to get a better view of the extraordinary sight.

Michael, of course, was oblivious to the stir he was causing. It seemed to him the most natural thing in the world, nothing more than a father taking his daughter for a stroll on a nice spring morning. Why should anyone give them so much as a second glance?

Even April Simon, who was more or less prepared for the idea of Michael McCann and fatherhood, had to suppress a smile when she saw him wheeling his daughter into her cluttered shop.

"Good morning," he said sunnily. "Mathilda, say good morning to Mrs. Simon."

"Goo-mng."

"Close enough." With the flourish, Michael laid a fan of bills on the counter. "Just got paid for a highboy I made for a family in Charlottesville."

"I have some 1876 Philadelphia Exposition five-dollar golds," said April Simon. "I could be persuaded to let them go for a good price."

Michael stared at her blankly. "Gold coins? What on earth would I want with gold coins. I want toys."

"Toys?"

"Yes, toys. Playthings." He strode around the store, grabbing at toys indiscriminately. "I want rattles and dolls and miniature kitchen ranges and those brightly colored, scientifically designed educational toys from Scandinavia that are supposed to stimulate and challenge your child so much she'll grow up to be the next Mozart without the personality problems, or Beethoven with hearing. That's what I want."

April nodded and smiled. She knew what it was like to want to buy your child everything in sight—every parent did. But she had also learned from experience that moderation when the child was still a baby would save Michael a lot of trouble down the road.

"Hope you don't mind my saying so, but you should think of yourself once in a while. You work hard for your money, so treat yourself. Can't hurt, right?"

With a flourish, Michael waved the rattle he was holding under her nose. "This is for me."

"Why? What on earth would you want that thing?" April was so unused to Michael making jokes that she did not recognize one when he did. She thought he was serious and, given his decidedly odd turn of mind, he could well have been in deadly earnest.

"I was kidding."

"Well, *that's* a first." Michael McCann's first, feeble foray into humor! It was amazing how having a child could change a man.

There was one set of purchases Michael McCann did not have to make: the various pieces of baby furniture necessary for the child's room. For a few weeks he put aside all his money-making commissions and dedicated himself to making the finest, handcrafted crib, high chair and playpen outside of the museum of American furniture in Williamsburg, Virginia.

Mathilda watched him as he worked, watching intently as he stood planing and finishing a piece of fine ash that would be part of her crib. Cautious to a fault, Michael had her eyes protected from flying wood chips by strapping a huge pair of oversized safety goggles on her head. She looked like a very small, golden-haired alien, but she didn't seem to mind. She watched and chattered to herself in her own private baby patois, though she occasionally addressed a word or two to Michael in a more comprehensible language.

One word, though, brought him to a sudden halt. He whipped around and stared at his daughter. "What? What was that? What did you say?"

She pointed at him and giggled. "Dad-dy."

Michael smiled and a warm glow spread through him. He returned to his work. "Daddy," he said, as if tasting the word. "That's me."

Of course, Michael McCann was not the only citizen of Burrows busily building his life. John Newland—The Honorable John Newland, Congressman—was about to add yet another glorious page to his perfect résumé.

He and Keating were saddling up for yet another polo game, Newland whistling brightly as he cinched tight the girth strap under the belly of the horse.

"You seem in a good mood lately," said Keating.

"I should be," said Newland. He put a foot in a stirrup and swung himself into the saddle. "Nancy Lammeter has said yes." It was all he could do to suppress a self-satisfied smirk.

"What?" Keating had been taken completely by surprise. "What did you say? She said yes?" He thrust out his hand. "Congratulations! Can I tell people?"

Newland shook his head. "Not yet."

"Can I tell my wife?"

John Newland deflected the question. "How's that McCann thing working out? He's taken possession of the child I gather." He spoke as if Michael had picked up an advantageous lease on a rental car.

"Yes," said Keating. "He's named her Mathilda. God help us."

John Newland laughed. "Children have to grow up to resent their parents for something. Might as well be the name Mathilda. . . . Have you found out any more about the paternity?"

"I got a Fed Ex from Richmond today. Nothing on who the real father is. You want us to keep looking?"

"No point in that," said Newland. "McCann seems decent enough and interested in the welfare of . . . Mathilda. Besides which, we have the whole community to watch over her."

Keating climbed into the saddle and gave his horse a loose rein. The animal clip-clopped slowly toward the polo field. "Why are you so interested in helping this guy? And don't tell me it's because he's a voter."

It was time to deflect this line of questioning and get back to the subject of his impending marriage. "You can tell your wife after Nancy tells her dad."

Keating forgot all about asking John about his interest in Michael and Mathilda McCann. He leered at Newland. "Hey, John, you been sleeping with her?"

"Mind your manners," said John Newland, spurring his horse out onto the field.

* * *

The game was fast and hard fought, but John Newland once again emerged victorious, having scored three of the four goals. Keating watched Newland leave the field, leading his mount by the bridle and walk over to Nancy Lammeter. They looked like a perfect couple, posing for an advertisement for something expensive—diamonds, perhaps, or champagne or a credit card that they wouldn't give to just anybody. Tall, dark, and handsome John Newland; beautiful, faultlessly dressed Nancy Lammeter, a polo pony—there was even a Mercedes in the background, almost brand new, a replacement for the one Tanny had destroyed.

Keating shook his head and wondered if success could ever be so constant as to be monotonous, if triumph could ever become something routine and mundane.

The road from the polo grounds to the Newland mansion ran by Michael McCann's house and John Newland slowed down as they passed. Michael was playing with Mathilda in the front yard, oblivious to the fact that he was being observed.

The little girl sat in the grass clapping her tiny hands as Michael sang at the top of his lungs.

"Ma-thild-da, Ma-thil-da You take-a my money and run to Venezuela!"

Nancy thought the whole scene charming. "That'll be you, one day," she said. "Children, children, children. They'll be hanging from the rafters."

John Newland nodded. "Anything, baby. Anything you want."

"That's what I want."

"You got it," he said, the car speeding up and pulling away from the happy sight.

Michael looked up just in time to see the car drive off, but he gave it no thought. He reached down to lift his daughter from the grass. As he leaned over he noticed something glittering on the ground, a small silver bracelet, a trinket that had lain there all winter, covered by the heavy blanket of snow. He put it in his pocket and realized that Mathilda was sitting in the exact spot where her mother had died.

11

As time passed, the sight of Michael and Mathilda became commonplace and people scarcely gave them a second glance when they made their weekly parade down Main Street. Not only had the spectacle become familiar, but attention had been turned elsewhere, toward a more exciting event, an occurrence that provided ample subject matter to jaw over in the Rainbow Bar. News of John Newland's impending wedding to Nancy Lammeter had galvanized the little town—the union of two local dynasties not being something that happened every day.

The wedding occupied everyone—except Michael McCann, who hardly even noticed it. He was preoccupied by—to his manner of thinking—far more important matters, like convincing his daughter that eating something as unappetizing as, say, unsalted mashed carrots was a good thing to do, not to say necessary to sustain life.

Like all children, Mathilda was pretty sure that if she got enough play under her belt, then things like food, water, sleep, and discipline were more or less useless, being nothing more than interruptions to far more important pursuits, such as the single-minded desire to put one of her feet in her mouth, or to see how much newspaper could be shredded in the shortest period of time.

As Mathilda became more mobile, Michael discovered that small children are among the swiftest creatures on the face of the earth. In addition to being amazingly fleet of foot, they also had an astoundingly accurate built-in tracking device which immediately locked on and honed in on the most hazardous substance, object or situation within a two-to-three mile radius. In addition to these two remarkable qualities, small children are possessed of a fearlessness that would daunt most soldiers. Secure in their sense of immortality, toddlers will waltz along the edge of disaster with the grace of ballroom dancers, thoroughly enjoying themselves while pushing parents ever closer to heart failure.

If Michael opened a can of varnish, for example, when he thought Mathilda was safe in her crib taking her afternoon nap, it would take under five minutes for her to awaken, climb stealthily out of her crib and make for the pot of poison. Inevitably, he would discover her at the last possible moment, just as she was about to take a deep gulp, or plunge into the toxic stew headfirst.

Constant vigilance was required, but not even a father as devoted as Michael could provide it. When he settled down to work, he made sure that his daughter was set up nearby with a set of blocks or wooden toys he had made for her, but as he became absorbed in his task, he would forget about her. Then he'd look up and she would have vanished.

A thousand gruesome scenarios would flash through his mind and he would discover that he could instantly recall every single missing child horror story he has ever heard. Consequently, when he would find Mathilda doing something no more dangerous than say, methodically emptying every tube of toothpaste in the house, he was inclined to forgive rather than punish.

However, Michael knew he had to do something to make Mathilda more secure and he hit upon a simple solution. He bought a twelve-foot-long piece of three-inch-wide satin ribbon. Every morning, he tied one end to the leg of his workbench and the other end to Mathilda's ankle. She could wander, but she could never quite make it out of Michael's field of vision. It was a situation that seemed to satisfy both father and daughter.

Michael's attempts to amuse Mathilda were equally inventive. He would prowl April Simon's store looking for odds and ends that he thought might divert his daughter. When she was only a year-to-eighteen-months old, simple things pleased her immensely—commonplace items, skillfully handled, could provide hours of amusement: a bathrobe, a paper bag, or even something as simple as a balloon could send Mathilda into paroxysms of laughter. As time passed and Mathilda grew older, though, her tastes became more refined and Michael had to work harder to keep her entertained.

He ransacked April Simon's store. "I need *something* that will amuse a three-year-old."

"How about my income?" said April Simon.

"Very funny . . ." The weather balloon that April had acquired a couple of years before still sagged in the corner of her shop. The weather balloon collectors had not, as she had hoped, come calling. Michael examined the object critically. Mathilda had always enjoyed a good balloon when she was smaller. Maybe it was time for an upgrade. . . . Besides, he had an idea that he knew Mathilda would really go for.

"You've had that balloon for a long time. How much do you want for it?"

"Hundred bucks," said April Simon without hesitation.

"Will you take five?"

"Sold," she said firmly.

"Where can I get gas for this?" He wondered if the Burrows hardware store would be able to provide him with enough helium to fill the bright red bag.

"Just eat what I eat," said April.

It took a while for him to scare up enough helium gas to inflate the balloon and another couple of days to fashion a harness out of some old leather belts and canvas webbing he had lying around his cabin. The next step was to actually try out the contraption, a skeptical Mrs. Simon, her son, Lawrence, and Mathilda looking on.

Michael made a running start, dashing across his front yard, the balloon quivering in the wind behind him. As he gained speed the lift from the balloon kicked in, until Michael's feet were barely touching the ground. At the end of his fifty-yard sprint, he took a flying leap, and soared ten feet into the air and, like an astronaut walking on the moon, he landed some twenty feet away. The instant his toes touched the ground, he pushed himself off anew, again flying into the air.

"Unbelievable!" gasped April Simon.

Lawrence and Mathilda were laughing and clapping their hands, running along behind Michael, desperately trying to catch up with him. Reaching the far side of the lawn, Michael managed an awkward, ungainly turn and hit the ground, bouncing back toward his audience.

"What do you think?" Michael shouted.

"If I hadn't seen it, I wouldn't have believed it," April called.

"Take me for a ride!" Lawrence yelled. "I wanna a ride! I wanna fly!"

Michael had anticipated such a request. He hit the ground and held on—the balloon fought gravity, trying to yank Michael skyward—and buckled an old motorcycle crash helmet to Lawrence's head.

"Let's go!" Michael grabbed Lawrence in his arms and together they went bounding off across the lawn, the child squealing in delight.

"My turn!" howled Mathilda. "It's my turn!"

"Okay." He swooped down to earth and gently placed Lawrence on the ground. Michael paused only long enough to jam the helmet on his daughter's head, buckling it under her chin and then took to the sky again.

Michael spent the rest of the afternoon hopping back and forth across his lawn, giving rides to the two children until his arms ached.

April watched and shook her head. It was hard to tell who was more delighted with this new, bizarre invention, the children or Michael McCann.

But even more amazing than this peculiar contraption was the change that had come over Michael with the advent of fatherhood. It was hard to believe that this small child, a child whom no one wanted, could have made for such unexpected change. Single-handed, she had succeeded in transforming a cold, sullen man into this laughing loon, a happy man with a weather balloon strapped to his back.

No one else in Burrows witnessed Michael McCann becoming airborne because the adventure with the balloon coincided with the social event of the season, the wedding of Nancy Lammeter and John Newland. Almost the entire town turned out to witness the marriage, the crowd lining the sidewalk around the picture-perfect Episcopal church on the Burrows village green.

Nancy wore a creation specially designed for the wedding, and John Newland was decked out in a cutaway morning coat and striped pants, the traditional uniform worn by members of the upper class on happy occasions like this one. The wedding ceremony was conducted with all the pomp and solemnity called for. There was a choir and fabulous flowers and the service was conducted by the bishop himself.

Dad was relieved to hear that John and Nancy had recited their vows properly. It seemed like a good omen.

The reception, held at the Burrows Polo Club was the high point of the social year. The guest list was as brilliant as the celebration, with the cream of hunt country aristocracy turning out to salute the union of two of its charter families. The champagne was vintage and unlimited, the buffet tables were spread with acres of exquisite food. The merrymaking lasted into the night, and even after the happy couple had departed for their Venice honeymoon, their guests continued to exclaim over how magnificent it had all been.

No one noticed—or if they had, did not remark upon it—that John Newlands's closest living relative, Tanny, was nowhere to be seen.

12

Venice worked its magic. Nancy Lammeter-Newland returned from her honeymoon pregnant. The realization that they were going to have a child took a while to sink in, but gradually, John and Nancy found that they were changing. Their attitude toward their own lives underwent a profound transformation, shifting from a subtle self-absorption to a focus on the life they had created. Life went on as usual, of course, but now they were living it for their child.

But there was business to attend to. John Newland commuted to Washington five days a week, attending to business in Congress, Monday through Friday, returning home to Burrows on the weekends. A house full of servants notwithstanding, Nancy found her husband's absences hard to bear, and her burden was made more difficult by the fact that Newland continued to conduct business during his brief sojourns at home.

A congressman uses his weekends to work with his constituents, to entertain prominent citizens in his district, and to continue the never-ending process of raising money for the next political campaign.

The Newlands had visitors virtually every weekend, as well as a never-ending round of dinner parties, cocktail parties, and the inevitable house guests who came up from Washington to discuss House business with John. The natural exhaustion that accompanies pregnancy was compounded by a fretfulness and anxiety, a gnawing fear within Nancy that she was not performing up to the high standards her husband expected of her.

Nancy seemed unable to prevent herself from working too hard. The servants of the Newland residence were old hands at running and organizing a busy household, and Nancy could have safely left the operation of the house to them, but she couldn't let go.

As a dinner party approached one weekend, Nancy buzzed about the kitchen, fussing and worrying, and generally getting in the way of her extremely efficient cook, Esther.

"I don't think we have enough salmon," Nancy said, bustling about the kitchen. She peered at the two, huge freshly poached salmon while Esther worked at mincing a mound of parsley for the cold *sauce verte* that would accompany the main course. The food processor on the kitchen counter hummed, beating egg yolks and olive oil into fresh mayonnaise.

"We have enough, Mrs. Newland," said the cook. "More than enough."

"I think we should send for more," insisted Nancy. She put a hand to her belly, as if to comfort the baby within. Then she paled slightly.

"Really no need to do that, ma'am. I'm sure we have enough. You've got six guests coming and two large salmon." Esther returned to her sauce. "As it is, I think you're going to have leftovers and you'll be eating them for a week, at the very least." Her back to her boss, Esther did not see Nancy sit down heavily in one of the kitchen chairs.

"Why don't you go rest, Mrs. Newland? Everything down here in the kitchen will take care of itself. Only *you* can take care of that little baby, you know."

Nancy nodded and wandered outside. She was feeling woozy and ill and she hoped that a little fresh air would clear her head. Even though it was late afternoon, she felt a bout of morning sickness coming on—whoever named it morning sickness had never been pregnant. It could strike at any moment of the day or night.

But this was something different. Nancy felt a sharp pain, a deep interior pain, as if a hot wire had suddenly been threaded through her belly.

"Esther . . . ?" Nancy felt her knees give way under her and the grass seemed to rush up toward her. Her brain reeled, as if she had been whirled in a circle and her vision blurred. Somewhere, far away, she heard Esther screaming for someone to call a doctor. . . .

* * *

Nancy lay in her hospital bed, as still as a statue, her pretty face drawn, haggard, and pale, her blond hair dull and lank. She scarcely looked at her husband when he came into the room, as if she was afraid of him, fearful of what he might say to her.

John took her hand and held it for a long time before speaking, as if they needed to reestablish contact before they could actually communicate.

Finally, he spoke. "We'll just try again," he said, turning his wife's head in his hands until they were looking into each other's eyes. "Think of the fun we'll have." He did his best to smile.

"I'm sorry," she said. Her voice was dry and hoarse, as if rusty from lack of use.

"Sorry? Don't ever say that to me," he said. "You have nothing to be sorry for. Nothing, understand?" He put his arms around her and hugged her close. "Please don't torture yourself. There's no reason to. No reason at all. What happened . . . it was nobody's fault."

Nancy let herself go, allowing herself to relax in her husband's strong arms. Tears started into her eyes, but her voice was strong. "John, you will have a child."

"Nancy . . ."—he smoothed her hair and tried to calm her—"don't worry about it."

But Nancy sat up, insistent. "You will have a child, John. That's a promise."

Michael McCann's day had begun as it always did. He got Mathilda up, fed and dressed her as usual, did a few routine chores around the house, and then got down to work. But before he turned his attention to the writing table he was making, he made sure that Mathilda was safe. He looped the red ribbon around his daughter's ankle and tethered the other end to the kitchen table, the way he always did, settling Mathilda on the floor near him with her toys and her coloring books.

The task at hand today was the completion of a delicate piece of boiserie, a carved frieze of acanthus leaves that ran down the legs of the desk Michael was making. It was tricky, complicated work, requiring a careful, steady hand, and absolute concentration. There was no margin for error—a slip of the chisel and the piece would be ruined beyond repair, wasting weeks of hard work.

Michael couldn't say how much time had passed when he looked up from his toil. It could have been an hour or only fifteen minutes—but it didn't matter. All that mattered was that Mathilda had taken advantage of his concentration. She had managed to get hold of a pair of scissors from the kitchen drawer, snipped through the ribbon, and had made her escape.

The house was still. A parent has a sixth sense about things like this and Michael knew in an instant that this time Mathilda's breakout was a serious one. The front door stood open and Michael was through it and outside in a flash.

His heart pounding, he raced across the lawn, praying that he would see his daughter playing unconcerned and unhurt in the grass, or with the weather balloon which bobbed next to the house. But she was nowhere to be seen.

Sick to his stomach and fighting a rising panic, Michael tried to calm himself and think rationally. Mathilda could be anywhere on the property and *he* had to be everywhere at once.

Mathilda, of course, was unaware of the torment she was causing her father. Sitting on the floor near her father was not her idea of a good time, but as her father had admonished on a dozen occasions, she was not to leave his sight—ever. Mathilda was not a willfully disobedient child, but she did have an insatiable curiosity about the world around her and she had the wile and cunning to escape to take a look at it.

Michael was so deeply immersed in his work that it was a very simple thing to get the scissors and cut through her leash. Then, on tiptoes, she stole out of the house.

The front lawn was too boring for her. She knew every inch of it, every contour and hiding place. It was what lay in the woods and beyond that interested her. She toddled along the path that ran through the forest, crossed the main road, oblivious to any danger from traffic, and climbed the gravel shoulder on the far side. At the summit of the little rise, Mathilda paused and looked out over the gray waters and rocky shoreline of Stone Lake.

Stone Lake was not a lake at all, not in the geological sense that is, but a flooded quarry, a leftover legacy of the granite-cutting trade that had once thrived in the neighborhood.

There were all kinds of rumors and legends attached to Stone Lake, myths that had been told in the region for decades. People said that the lake was bottomless or that there was a labrynthine system of tunnels and blow holes in the lake bed that could cause strange whirlpools and eddies which could suck an unwary bather down into the inky black depths.

The bottom was said to be a jungle of thick vegetation, plants with tendrils like tentacles that held the skeletons of a dozen bodies, drunks and bums who had tumbled into the lake in the dark. The children of the neighborhood frightened and thrilled each other with tales of the Stone Lake monster, a distant cousin of the freak of nature that inhabited Loch Ness.

In truth, Stone Lake *was* a dangerous place, but for far less colorful reasons. In parts the waters were deep and cold, though some were just deep enough to hide dangerous reefs and outcroppings of hard rock. The most hazardous feature of the quarry were the sheer sides—slick, vertical cliffs of wet rock. Those unlucky enough to tumble into the water would have to claw and scratch a way out, battling the steep slope, while fighting the twin dangers of exposure and exhaustion.

This is where Mathilda McCann found herself, at the very edge of the slippery crag, peering, eyes full of curiosity, into the placid gray waters. It was a sunny day, a light breeze blowing, and right then Stone Lake looked like a pleasant, unthreatening, curiously inviting place. Mathilda took a step closer to the edge of the precipice, staring down into the water twenty feet below her, a bit of the cliff crumbling away under her little boots.

Just when it seemed inevitable that she would plunge into the water, Michael came bounding over the rise, the weather balloon strapped to his back. In a single hop he pounced on his daughter and grabbed her in his arms and sprung away from the edge, hauling Mathilda into the air. The little girl squealed in delight at her sudden ascent, thinking that her father was just playing with her.

When they were safely away from the edge of the cliff, Michael landed and hugged his daughter close. He didn't know whether to laugh or cry, to scold her or to smother her with thankful kisses and praise for her bravery—so he did all of those things all at once.

"Mathilda!" he yelped. "You almost gave me a heart attack! Are you crazy to go wandering off like that! Never, never, *never* go near the lake. Ever!" He shifted gears abruptly. "Oh, honey, I was *so* worried! How could you do a thing like that? Are you okay? You must have been scared to death!"

"No," said Mathilda. "Take me for another ride, Daddy. Please."

By the time they had bounced back to the cottage, Michael had stopped trembling, but he realized that he had a serious problem. Plainly the ribbon was not going to work anymore, so a better system would have to be devised to keep Mathilda in her place—literally.

Michael turned to his guru in all matters of child-raising, April Simon. The moment they got back to the house he explained his predicament to her.

April was firm. "Well, Michael, you have only one alternative. You just have to punish her."

Michael gulped. "Punish her?"

"You have to, otherwise she'll never learn."

"I can't do that."

"It's your duty to," said April. "It's the only way for her to learn what she can and cannot do. It's the only way for her to learn what's best for her."

Michael could be just as firm as April Simon. "Well, I can't spank," he said matter-of-factly. "If that's what you're going to suggest, then you can just forget it."

"Nobody said anything about having to spank her," April replied. "Use your head, Michael, there are other ways of disciplining a child, you know."

"Like what?"

"Use your imagination. What did your parents do when you were bad?"

"On those very rare occasions that I misbehaved," he said, "I . . . er, got spanked."

"Well think of something else."

"What am I supposed to do? Behead her teddy bear? That would traumatize her."

April laughed. "Well, you better think of something, because the way you're going now, that kid is headed straight for the loony bin."

"Thanks a lot."

"I call 'em as I see 'em, Michael."

"Then tell me what to do. I need some advice here. I've never done this before."

"Well, with Lawrence, I would make him sit in a corner for one hour."

"An hour?" That seemed like an awfully long time to him. In general, Mathilda seemed to be incapable of sitting still for more than five minutes at a time and even that was something of a stretch.

"Not one minute less," she said sternly. "It's not supposed to be fun." The last few words were indistinct, as if April had turned away from the phone while speaking. "Michael? Wait a minute, Lawrence wants to speak to you."

Next came the muffled sound of the phone being passed, then the high-pitched voice of April Simon's six-year-old son speaking earnestly.

"Mister McCann?"

"Yes, Lawrence."

"About making Mathilda sit in the corner . . ."

"Yes?"

"Don't do it," said Lawrence passionately. "Look what it's done to me."

Michael hung up, more confused than ever. But he supposed there was something to April's suggestion.

"Okay," he said to Mathilda, dragging a kitchen chair into the corner of the room, "for the crime of going too near the quarry, you are sentenced to sit in the corner for . . ." An hour seemed too long. "You'll have to sit there for twenty minutes or for as long as it takes me to make lunch."

Mathilda shrugged. "Okay," she said, climbing into the chair and settling herself there.

"Well," Michael thought, "that's that."

He immediately set about putting together two sandwiches for their lunch. Michael did his best not to look in Mathilda's direction as he went about his task, even when she started singing to herself and giggling about some private joke or other. Her father glanced at the clock. Scarcely a minute had passed and yet it seemed like an hour. He hoped that sitting in the corner was as much a punishment for his daughter as it was for him.

It took only a few more minutes to make the sandwiches and to lay the table. But Michael could not stand the torture for a moment longer.

"Okay," he said, hoping he sounded stern yet forgiving, "you're free. Come and have your lunch."

"Yes, Daddy," she said. She hopped off the chair and took her place at the kitchen table. Michael sat next to her.

"That was very naughty. Going to the lake like that. You know that, don't you?"

Mathilda swallowed a mouthful of sandwich and nodded. "Uh-huh."

"And you'll never do it again will you?"

Mathilda shook her curls vigorously. "Uh-uh."

"And you know it was very, very dangerous."

"Yes, I do, Daddy."

"Good," said Michael, satisfied that he had set his daughter on the road to self-discipline.

They ate in silence for a moment, but Michael couldn't quite let the subject drop—he rather enjoyed playing the role of a strict daddy.

"You understand that if you step out of line again, then I'll be forced to punish you."

"Yes, Daddy."

"Good," he said briskly. "Are you finished your lunch?"

"Yup."

"What would you like to do now?"

Mathilda jumped to her feet and clapped her hands. "I know!" she said brightly.

"What?"

"I'll show you!"

She toddled across the room and climbed back into her punishment chair and began her singing and giggling again.

Michael shook his head wearily. Mathilda never ceased to surprise him.

13

In five short years, Mathilda went from being a baby to becoming, in Michael's eyes, a self-assured young woman—who just happened to look like a cute, blond six-year-old.

Maybe it was that buried somewhere in her memory was the faint image of her hard start in life that gave her that sense of poised self-possession, a feeling that things could never be as bad as they had been.

Mathilda was fearless and confident in everything, in her dealings with adults and children—bold and brave in everything, it seemed, except when facing the first day of school, that greatest of childhood nightmares.

Michael delivered Mathilda to the Burrows Junior School on a fresh autumn day, leading her by the hand into the schoolyard. He sort of hated himself for it, but Michael found himself spouting all of the distortions, falsehoods, and bromides that his own parents had inflicted on *his* first day of school all those years ago.

"This is school. You'll like it."

Mathilda eyed the building and then looked at her father suspiciously.

"Really," he insisted. "It's fun. Truly. You'll learn lots of . . . stuff." Michael thought about his days as a teacher and how hard he had tried to make school pleasant. He hoped that someone was still trying.

"Honest?" she asked skeptically. Mathilda was no fool. If getting an education was supposed to be so much fun, then why had so many dark rumors circulated about it in the Burrows preschool set?

"Yeah," he said, hating himself. "Honest."

"We'll see about *that*."

Michael was relieved and turned to go, leaving his daughter in the middle of a crowd of her new schoolmates. "Well, have fun!" he said as brightly as he could. It was no picnic for him either. He found that there was something dispiriting about the thought of returning to an empty house.

Michael started edging toward the gate. "Have a nice day, dear."

To Michael's horror, Mathilda began to sniffle. The closer he got to the gate, the more intense the sniffling became. By the time he was on the sidewalk, she was bawling at the top of her voice. The crying cut through him like a knife and he knew that there was nothing he could to shut it out. Michael raced back to his daughter's side, kneeled down next to her, and wiped her tears with his handkerchief.

"No, no, honey," he said. "You don't get it.

This is school. I'll pick you up when it's over." He tried to make the process as clear as possible. "I come and pick you up and we go back home together. Got it?"

Mathilda wasn't buying any of it. She continued to wail, crying as if her heart had been broken in two, as if she had been cruelly betrayed by the one person in the world she trusted without reservation.

Michael was desperate to make her stop crying, but just didn't know how. School, as any sane adult knew, seemed to be a life sentence when viewed from a child's point of view. How could he explain that going to school, like not falling in Stone Lake, was an important, essential part of growing up.

A shadow fell across them. "You her father?"

Michael looked up. Standing in the schoolyard was Mrs. Latham, the supervisor of the junior school, a well known figure in the Burrows area.

Michael struggled to his feet. "Well," he said sheepishly, "she adopted me."

Mathilda had downgraded the wailing to mere sniffles again, and she was hiccuping and gasping for air as she fought to control her sobs. The little girl still looked like the very picture of misery. "Mrs. Latham, I wonder if I could have a word with you for a moment?"

"Of course . . ."

Taking the administrator by the arm, Michael walked her out of earshot and the two had a hurried, whispered conference on the edge of the schoolyard.

Mrs. Latham listened to his proposal, but she looked dubious, to say the least. "Mr. McCann, this is most unusual. I don't really see how I could allow it."

"Mrs. Latham, consider the alternative." Michael pointed to Mathilda. The little girl stood in the middle of the schoolyard, crying and looking like a study in abject sorrow. Looking at her, a piece of Michael's heart crumbled.

Mrs. Latham wasn't unmoved either. "Okay," she said, "we'll try it."

"Great!"

"But only for a few days," she said. "Then we try the old-fashioned method."

"Fine."

When school session began that morning, there were eighteen six-year-olds in the first grade class—and a carpenter who was just pushing forty. Michael was squeezed into one of the tiny kid-sized desk chairs which he had parked in the far corner of the classroom. He managed not to show it, but Michael felt sort of queasy—this was the first time he had spent any time in a school building since his betrayal by his former wife. The smell of chalk and the drone of teacher's voices echoing in the passageway brought back memories, but, curiously, memories not as painful as he had expected. Mathilda had changed his life so much that she had even managed to salve that ancient wound.

Periodically, Mathilda glanced over at her father, saw that he was still there and returned to the fingerpainting or story telling, or whatever it was that happened to be on the school syllabus.

The second day of school, Michael returned with his daughter, this time placing his desk and chair very close to the door. Mathilda continued to be reassured, suspecting nothing, and gradually settling into the cadence and patterns of first-grade life. She discovered that her father had not been lying about school—it *was* fun.

Mathilda was having so much fun, in fact, that she didn't take it too hard when Michael moved his desk out of the classroom altogether, placing it in the corridor. From time to time, she peeked out through the window in the door, just checking that he was still there.

By the third day, when he quietly stole out of school in the hour before lunch, Mathilda hardly noticed.

Michael drove home happy, delighted to find that there seemed to be a solution to each and every problem parenting presented.

Not being a parent presented a completely different set of problems, difficulties not so easily resolved. The Newland mansion, in contrast to the happy McCann cottage, was quiet and somber, melancholy in the wake of Nancy's miscarriage. The normally ebullient John Newland was quiet now, given to moody silences and long bouts of introspection.

Nancy found him in the study, sitting behind his desk, some figures scratched on a pad in front of him, but he wasn't working. Newland was staring out of the window, as if examining the bright day for defects. He scarcely looked up when his wife came into the room.

"You all right?" Nancy asked.

Newland nodded. "Yeah, yeah," he said softly. "Just thinking, that's all."

Nancy smiled wryly. "That I could tell. What are you thinking about."

"I was just thinking about my brother, Tanny. Just wondering where he might be."

"Not even a postcard in all this time," said Nancy with a dismissive shake of her head. "He really doesn't care about you, John."

"I did some figuring," said John Newland, gesturing toward the figures in front of him. "McCann's coins were worth about forty thousand when Tanny took off. If he used his head for once and held on to them, then they would be worth around ninety thousand, maybe more. . . ."

"That much? I'm surprised." Nancy had trouble imagining that the down-at-the-heels furniture maker could be worth so much money.

"I gather McCann always bought quality. That's a good investment strategy—if you can afford it." John Newland shook his head and smiled. "Tanny could have learned something from him, but he could never hold on to money. I'm sure he's gone through every penny by now—and he's probably in debt to boot."

Nancy looked puzzled. "What are you talking about? What are you trying to say?"

"He's always been trouble," John said, his

voice cold. "If one day he decided to come back . . . I think it would be trouble. A *lot* of trouble."

"He can't cause you trouble, John. He's a face. He'd be up on charges and there's nothing you or anyone else could do about it."

John Newland laughed bitterly. "That's great. That's all I need, a brother in the hoosegow. How's that going to look to the voters?"

Nancy stood behind her husband and rubbed his neck and shoulders, trying to release the tension she could feel knotted into his muscles.

"Don't worry about it, John. Please. We have more important things to think about." Her tone of voice made clear that she was talking about their next attempt to start a family of their own.

John Newland sighed, exasperated. He knew what was coming next. He tried to busy himself with some of the papers on his desk. "I'm thinking of developing some housing south of town. . . . I have to get the area rezoned for residential. Of course, it would mean draining Stone Lake, but that—"

Nancy did not care about such plans. "I'm having lunch with Diane Green tomorrow," she said. "You know they adopted three kids."

John looked sharply at his wife. "Adoption?"

"John, John . . . They adopted three kids and it turned out great. We could do it, too."

Newland turned back to the papers. "Nancy, I have this plan to get off the ground and there's an election to worry about."

"There will always be an election," she said, shaking her head sadly. "Always . . ."

* * *

When John Newland needed to be alone with his thoughts, he saddled up one of his horses and went for a ride on his property. He told himself that he wanted to inspect the land on the south side of his estate, the area he hoped to subdivide and build upon, but the truth of the matter was that he wanted to get out of the house, to escape Nancy's entreaties that he consider adopting a child. He was dead set against adoption, but despite his polished politician's way with words, he could not think of a way to tell her of his opposition without sounding cold, blunt, and unreasonable.

John Newland could scarcely admit his reasons for resistance to himself. To him a child was more than just a bundle of joy. In this day and age it sounded odd and anachronistic to think of having a child for dynastic reasons, but he couldn't help it. Any ambitions he held for himself would be doubled for his child. If the father could not ascend to the very top, then the son—or daughter—surely would. And when that happened, the child had to be pure Newland flesh and blood.

But there was another reason and it could shake the foundations of his marriage. *He* knew that he could father a child and it disturbed him more than he cared to admit that any fault must lie with Nancy. If she could not carry a baby to term, he would not gloss over her inability by adopting a strange child. He could not take the chance of bestowing the Newland name on an infant who might turn out to be . . . damaged goods.

Despite his deep and rather dark thoughts, he became aware of a sound, a low mournful dirge that mirrored the gloom of his musings. Newland rein his horse to a halt and listened for a moment, then a smile erased the troubled look from his face. The mournful tune was the "Song of the Volga Boatman" and it was being sung by a group of children who were wending their way through the woods, bearing a pizza box on their shoulders, as if the pizza had died and they were pallbearers. One of the children was Mathilda.

John Newland spurred his horse and rode over to the little gathering, stopping a few yards away. He leaned on the pommel of his saddle and watched the children.

Mathilda stopped and stared—but not at the man, at his horse.

"Hi, Mathilda," John Newland called. "What are you kids doing here?"

"Mouse burial," she explained. "We found a dead mouse and we're giving him a decent burial." Interesting though the mouse funeral may have been, it could not compete with a real live horse. Mathilda could scarcely take her eyes from the animal. She walked over and gingerly patted the soft nose. The horse snorted and nuzzled into her hand.

"You like horses?" asked John Newland

"I *love* horses," she said emphatically.

The mouse requiem continued in the background, the children going through "The Song of the Volga Boatman'' for the fortieth or fiftieth time.

''How did the mouse die?''

''It was run over by a car,'' explained Mathilda. ''That's why we're burying it in a pizza box. Flattened, you know?''

''I see,'' said Newland.

''I'm kidding.''

''I see. I think.''

Mathilda shrugged. ''Actually, a cat got it. It really wasn't anyone's fault. Just one of those things.''

John Newland laughed and turned his horse. ''Well, have a nice burial.''

''Well, we're trying but it's hard.'' Mathilda trotted off to rejoin the last rites for the mouse, while John Newland spurred his horse, cantering lightly across the clearing. However, before he plunged back into the wood, he stopped, turned in his saddle to catch one last glimpse of his daughter and her friends at such serious play.

The McCann household was growing more and more chaotic with the passing of every day. There is no more potent recipe for mayhem than the combination of a six-year-old and a puppy—and Mathilda absolutely *had* to have a puppy.

Michael did his best to accommodate the new addition to his little family, even going so far as to cut a puppy trapdoor in the front door of the house. He fed the dog, walked him, made him chew toys, and generally tried to make the puppy feel welcome. Mathilda played with him for hours on end, romping with the animal, frolicking all over the house.

Mathilda was not the most gentle of playmates, but the puppy didn't seem to mind—he could take or leave Michael, but he loved his little friend to distraction.

Mathilda did *not* love her nightly reading lessons, which Michael insisted on conducting each evening after dinner. Father and daughter sat side by side on the couch, the puppy on the floor nearby busily chewing on a leftover block of wood, absorbed in the business of reducing it to a puddle of saliva-covered pulp as quickly as possible.

"Okay," said Michael opening a book, "let's get started." He read precisely, enunciating every word. "The cat is on the mat." He smiled at his daughter. "Now you try."

Mathilda frowned as she took the book. "The cat is on the mat."

"The cat is *off* the mat," said Michael.

Mathilda rolled her eyes. "This is so dumb."

He could hardly believe his ears. "This? Dumb?" He smacked the cover of the book. "The cat is on the mat? This is a classic, you know. Cat . . . on mat. The brevity, the elegance—it's beautiful."

Mathilda folded her arms across her chest. "I'm six and I'm bored," she said emphatically.

"All right, all right," he said, going to his small library. "I know what you'll like . . ." He ran his finger along the line of books on his shelf.

"I doubt it."

Michael pulled a volume down. "Lewis Carroll."

"Never heard of him."

Michael refused to be put off by his daughter's lack of enthusiasm.

He opened the book. "Jabberwocky," he announced dramatically. Then he began to read. " 'Twas brillig and the slithy toves did gyre and gimble in the wabe; all mimsy were the borogroves and the mome raths outgrabe.' "

Mathilda blinked, not quite sure what she had heard, then began to chortle. "That's pretty good, Daddy. Better than the cat on the mat, anyway."

"But there's more . . . 'Beware the Jabberwock, my son, the jaws that bite, the claws that catch . . . beware the jubjub bird and shun the frumious bandersnatch . . .' "

"The *what*?"

"You know, the frumious bandersnatch," said Michael casually, as if his daughter probably ran into one every day of the week.

Mathilda laughed and clapped her hands. "Read some more, Daddy."

"You try," he said, pointing out the first word.

She read hesitantly. "Beware the Ja—" It was a word far more difficult than cat or mat.

"Jab-ber-wock," said Michael slowly, coaxing her along. "Ja-Buh-wock. Buh. Remember the 'bee' sound."

Mathilda nodded. " 'Beware the Jabberwock, my son . . .' "

". . . the jaws that bite . . ."

". . . the jaws that bite, the claws that catch!"

"Great!" said Michael. "Really terrific!"

"Beware the Jubjub bird, and shun the . . ."

"Frumious."

"Frumious—" She took a long hard look at the last word, silently sounding it out. Then: "Bandersnatch."

"Perfect!"

"Let me try again."

"From the top."

She cleared her throat. " 'Twas brillig and the slithy toves did gyre and gimble in the wabe . . .' "

They went through "Jabberwocky" a half a dozen times more, then moved on to selections from *Alice in Wonderland* and *Alice Through the Looking Glass* as well as all of *The Hunting of the Snark* and *The Walrus and the Carpenter*. They read deep into the night until Mathilda began to nod off in the middle of *You Are Old Father William*. The puppy, not a devotee of nonsense verse, had dozed off hours ago.

Gently, Michael lifted his little girl in his arms and carried her to her bed, tucking her in without waking her. He moved quietly around the house, tidying up and turning off lights, locking the front door, putting the house to bed, before retiring for the night himself.

Before turning out the kitchen light he noticed that Mathilda had discovered the old hiding place, the secret compartment in the kitchen table where he had concealed his coins. The little space was now stuffed with Mathilda's toys, a couple of dolls that were as precious to her as his money had once been to him. He smiled and glanced toward Mathilda's bed. How much more he valued his daughter than those dead coins.

"I'm not your real father," he whispered. "But I love you more than your real father did."

14

Mathilda had fun with the poems of Lewis Carroll, but life around the McCann house wasn't always as . . . educational. There were times when Michael *had* to get important work done, such as the time an unexpected order came in from Mrs. John Newland for a chest of drawers. Given that he was the Newland's tenant—and they hadn't raised the rent since he moved in—he felt that he had to put work aside and get to their commission immediately. This left Mathilda on her own for a while—and she found she didn't like it much.

She did her best to entertain herself for as long as she could, but when her ingenuity was exhausted, she fell back on that tried-and-true, never-fail, parent-annoying, attention-getting tactic: being still, quiet, and doing absolutely nothing except staring fixedly at the parent to be disturbed.

Michael did his best to ignore his daughter's gaze, continuing to work methodically at the chest of drawers, but he knew that she was getting the better of him. Finally he looked up and stared right back.

"What's the matter?"

Mathilda said nothing, contenting herself with nothing more than a noncommittal shrug.

Michael put down his plane and wiped his hands on a rag. "Come on, what's the matter? Tell me."

Mathilda had been a daughter long enough to know exactly how to keep her father off balance. "I can write really, really small," she said.

"Huh? What do you mean?"

"Look." She showed him a piece of paper torn from a school notebook. In the middle of the leaf was an almost perfect, half-inch-square black blot of ballpoint pen ink.

"What's that?"

"It's the name of every kid in my class. I wrote them all so small and close together, it's not really easy to read, I guess. Is it?"

Michael couldn't help but wonder how much time and effort had gone into this pointless exercise. "Good grief," he said, "I guess the question 'why' would be inappropriate, wouldn't it?"

Mathilda was admiring her handiwork. "I think it's kinda cool."

"Are you suffering from ennui?" he asked.

Mathilda considered the word for a moment. She had no idea what it meant, but she decided that she rather liked the sound of it. She nodded vigorously. "On-wee. That's me."

Luckily, Michael had the cure. During his reclusive period Michael McCann had missed the compact disc revolution. When he wanted music, he got it the old-fashioned way—the *very* old-fashioned way—from vinyl records. This was not such a bad thing because if he had converted to CDs, then the chances of his having the "Greatest Hits of Johnny Preston" would have been pretty slim. (In actual fact, Johnny Preston didn't have all that many hits—but "Running Bear" was definitely one of his greatest.)

Michael put the record on his ancient turntable and dropped the needle into the appropriate groove. Then he stood stock-still in the middle of the room.

The instant Preston began to sing, Michael started to dance a sort Indian dance—or, rather, what a former junior-school-teacher-turned-carpenter living in rural Virginia *imagined* to be an Indian dance. It must be said that he could lipsynch the words (and the back beat) to perfection.

Then Michael's stiff moves became sinuous and jazzy as Johnny Preston swung into a raucous rock and roll. (The ooga-ooga vanished as well.)

Mathilda plainly thought her father had lost his mind, but in a nice kind of way. She jumped in next to him and started capering about trying to learn the words as her father belted them out.

By the time they had gotten through all the travails of the star-crossed lovers and reached the end of the song, father and daughter had worked up a pretty ridiculous song and dance routine. They collapsed giggling on the couch.

"See," said Michael, "what did I tell you? No more dreaded ennui."

Mathilda, gasping for breath, managed to stop laughing just for a moment or two. "Dad?"

"Yeah?"

"Dad," she said, "we've got to get more, you know? It would promote good mental health."

She was right, of course. The very next night, Michael launched himself on what, for him, could only be called the social whirl. He took his daughter to a school choir recital and was surprised to see that April Simon was the unofficial choir mistress of the Burrows junior school. Even more surprising was the surpassing, transcendent lousiness of her singing ensemble.

It was their spectacularly awful rendition of "Three Coins in the Fountain" that pushed Michael over the edge and awakened the music teacher in his soul.

After the concert, Michael approached April Simon. "Maybe I should take over the choir," he suggested with a diffident little smile. He didn't want to offend the only friend he had and it was just possible that she thought there was absolutely nothing wrong with her ensemble.

April looked immensely relieved. "Oh *would* you? I try, but I'm just terrible!"

And that was that. Michael added the school choir to his duties and gradually, as he recalled his musical skills, the group went from being bad to mediocre to really quite good.

There was as much improvement in Michael's spirit as there was in his choir. He had forgotten how much he enjoyed teaching and the pure delight he felt in introducing children to the enchantments of music. And the choir paid a further dividend: Michael discovered that Mathilda had a lovely, if untrained, singing voice, a pure alto that was a welcome addition to the group.

Mathilda wasn't all that enthusiastic about being in the choir, but she went along with it to please her father. As she grew older, Mathilda found that the thing she *really* enjoyed was playing coed Little League baseball. In this particular pursuit, Michael had to take a backseat. He had never been much of a ball player, even in his youth, so he was content to attend every game cheering on his fledgling right fielder. His other diversion at the game was tormenting Charlie, the hot dog vendor.

"Charlie," he would say, "give me a tub of cole slaw."

"Don't have no cole slaw," Charlie said.

"Okay, how about a nice Welsh rarebit?"

Charlie sighed heavily, resigned to the constant ribbing. "No Welsh rarebit, Mr. McCann. No call for it."

"Okay," Michael deadpanned. "Then just give me a soufflé. You must have some kind of soufflé, right?"

"All I got is popcorn and hot dogs, Mr. McCann."

Michael considered this as if he had just been presented with a menu in a fine restaurant. "Hmmm. Popcorn . . . that could hit the spot. I'll take some, Charlie."

Charlie shoveled some popcorn into a box and handed it over. He seemed pleased that his weekly torment had come to an end. "There you go."

Michael took his popcorn and sat down next to April Simon in the bleachers.

"Popcorn?"

April took a handful. "How come you torture Charlie like that?"

"He likes it."

She shot Michael a skeptical, sideways glance. "Oh, sure, he does . . . You know," she said, "you better teach Mathilda some manners."

"What do you mean by that?"

"My boy Lawrence is crazy for her," said April. "But she won't have anything to do with him. He tries to talk to her and she ignores him."

Michael laughed. "That's not bad manners. That's what girls do to irritate boys. Besides, I don't think she's thinking about that stuff yet."

"But—"

"Wait. She's up."

Mathilda had stepped up to the plate, tapping her bat against her foot, knocking the caked dirt from her cleats, looking as if she was a major leaguer going into a tight seventh game of the World Series.

The third baseman, socked his glove and tensed, ready for any ball hit his way. "Hey, look! A girl! Easy out! Easy out!"

The rest of the infield took up the chatter. "C'mon. Get 'er out."

Mathilda's eyes narrowed and she looked down the third base line, drawing a bead on the third baseman, like a sniper looking down a gun barrel.

"C'mon, anyone can strike out a *girl*!" He put a nasty sneer on the last word, as if it was absolutely the worst insult he could think of.

For a moment or two, it looked as if the kid on third base was right. The pitcher reached back and threw two fast pitches—hot, smoking fastballs that blasted right through Mathilda's strike zone.

Being behind in the count didn't rattle her, and neither did the increased volume in the jeers, particularly the nasty taunts that were screeching in from third base. Mathilda stepped out of the batter's box, settled her batting helmet on her head, and took a couple of practice cuts with the bat. Then she stepped back into the batter's box.

"One more strike! C'mon! Strike 'er out."

The next pitch zoomed toward her, and her gaze fixed on the ball like a laser beam. She swung, putting all of her strength behind the bat—and she got all of the ball. There was a crack like a pistol shot and the ball soared toward the outfield fence. There was no doubt in anyone's mind that she had hit a home run. The crowd suddenly became very noisy; the opposing team became very quiet.

Mathilda stood at home plate, watching her ball sail out of the park, then she began her home run trot. But Mathilda being Mathilda, she didn't start for first base as tradition dictated, she headed for third, running the bases in reverse order, much in the style of the immortal Boston Red Sox Jimmy Piersall.

The third baseman had a sick little smile on his

face, watching as she jogged toward him and ready to run away if she decided to hit him. She didn't. She contented herself with a self-satisfied smirk.

"Not bad for a girl, huh?" she said as she trotted by on the way to second base.

Michael thought his chest was going to burst with pride. "She likes to do things her own way," he told April.

"I can see that."

After the game, Michael hooked up with his daughter and drove her home.

"That was a good game, kid."

"You did some good spectatoring, Pop."

"I do my best," he said. "Listen, I'm going to drop you off and then take that chest of drawers over to the Newlands' house. Okay?"

This piece of rather ordinary information almost made Mathilda levitate off the car seat. "The Newlands'! Can I go? I'm dying to see inside their house. I've heard they have gold salt shakers!"

Michael took his eyes off the road long enough to shoot a disapproving look at his daughter. "Hey, just because our salt shakers are made of linoleum, that's no reason to put them down."

"And they have a butler!" Mathilda yelped. "A real live butler."

"Oh, yeah," said Michael derisively, "a real live English butler. Here's what happens. They're sitting in the living room and Mrs. Newland rings a little bell"—he waved his wrist limply as if ringing a bell—"then the butler comes in." He rearranged his face to take on a solemn, stuffy mien. "Tea, suh?" he said in a very exaggerated English accent. "May I bring you a spot of tea?"

Mathilda laughed. "Oh, he does not."

"Just you wait and see."

Mathilda's eyes widened. "So I can go with you?"

"Of course," he said. "Just try not to break anything."

15

John Newland was having his monthly meeting with Roy Strong and Len Hamilton, his main political backers. It was not Newland's favorite event, but he recognized that this kind of back-room horse trading was part of political life and he had to live with it.

Randy Keating, who now functioned as John Newland's political secretary, sat discreetly in the background taking notes on the meeting. Nancy sat in, too, but she seemed distracted, paying little attention to the action in the center of the room. She found her husband's political career was coming to interest her less and less.

"We'd like a yes vote on the next house bill," said Strong. "Right down party lines. We're going to let them try and manipulate the swing votes, thinking the other side can get a swap on the tax credit. But we can expect your vote to be firm, right, John?"

John was tapping his pencil and glancing distractedly out the window. "Right."

"Now listen," said Hamilton, leaning forward. In contrast to Newland, these two big beefy old pols lived and breathed politics. Nothing in life interested them more. "We figure that you're gonna get a call from their whip—that son of a bitch—he'll be looking for a quid pro quo on the farm subsidies."

"Yes? So what?"

"We say play along," put in Strong. "Say anything. Then flip-flop at the last minute. He won't have enough votes if you switch late."

"Whatever," said Newland.

Keating saw the opportunity to bring up a matter of particular interest to his political master. "By the way, we're having difficulty getting permission to divert water from the quarry for John's housing project. . . ."

This bit of information ignited a spark of life in John Newland. He sat up straight and tossed aside his pencil. "Trouble? No, we're not."

"I'm afraid we are, John."

John Newland looked from Strong to Hamilton. "What the hell is going on here?"

"We're getting some flack, John. It'll all be worked out. Just be patient."

"Oh, I'll be patient. For about half an hour. You get me my zoning ordinance and you'll get your yes vote. No ordinance. No vote. Got it?"

Hamilton and Strong exchanged worried looks. Junior congressmen were not supposed to treat their party leaders like this. They were supposed to shut up and do what they were told. But both of the old hacks knew that John Newland didn't need them for reelection.

They had commissioned private polls of John

Newland's district and discovered that he was so popular that he would be reelected no matter what party platform he happened to support. They couldn't even squeeze him with promises of help in fund raising—he had more than enough of his own money to pay for an election in his district.

"I think I make myself clear," said Newland.

"You might say that," said Strong, doing his best to muster a smile.

John nodded curtly. "Good. If there is nothing else . . ."

Strong and Hamilton had the uneasy feeling that they were being dismissed by their own protegé. They didn't care for that at all. . . .

The instant the politicians left, Nancy came in from seeing them out, carrying a letter.

"Daisy's pregnant again," she announced, her face drawn and grim.

John grimaced. "She really knows how to rub it in, doesn't she? That will be her third child."

John Newland's words cut Nancy to the quick, and almost as they left his mouth, he felt ashamed for having caused her so much pain, so thoughtlessly.

"I'm sorry, darling . . . I really am." He did his best to sound contrite. "Maybe you need something to take your mind off things."

"I'm sorry, I—"

"Look, I've been talking to Keating. We're going to create some very nice lots. Would that interest you?"

"Interest me how?"

"Well, it's going to be a nice area and maybe we could put up a house on it. A new house, *our* house. The quarry has too much water; I could divert the water, sell it to myself, and make a lake out of it." He smiled warmly. "A house on a lake. It sounds nice doesn't it? We could look at the ducks all day."

"You would want to leave this house?" said Nancy. "Are you sure? Your family has lived here for generations. . . ." But John Newland wasn't listening. He was staring fixedly through the window, watching as Michael McCann's old pickup truck pulled to a halt in front of the house. Mathilda was clambering down from the passenger's side.

"John," said Nancy, "you've got to snap out of it. It's as if you're sleepwalking."

"Michael McCann and his daughter," he said, "what are they doing here?"

"Oh," said Nancy, going to the front door, "he must be here to deliver the chest of drawers I ordered."

Mathilda was already in awe of the Newland house, amazed at the long driveway, the carefully tended lawns, and the beautiful gardens. When Nancy opened the front door and the little girl caught a glimpse of the magnificent interior, all she could do was gasp.

"Wow!" she said, stepping into the marble-lined entrance hall.

"Hello, Michael, Mathilda."

"Hi, Mrs. Newland. Your house . . . it's *beautiful.*"

"I hope you don't mind me bringing her," said Michael. "She's never been here. . . ." That was not strictly true, of course. Mathilda was completely unaware that she had been there once before and Michael was glad that she couldn't remember anything of that terrible snowy night.

Nancy Newland kept the secret. She smiled sweetly. "No problem at all. Would you like to take a look around, Mathilda? I'll give you the guided tour."

"That would be great!"

Michael went off to unload the chest of drawers from his truck while Nancy led his daughter farther into the grand house. The mansion and the splendid possessions contained within it impressed Mathilda, but the richness did not intimidate her, nor did she feel particularly envious. Her own modest home was . . . well, home. The Newland mansion was a museum.

To her immense surprise, the Newlands *did* own a set of gold salt and pepper shakers, which she found a little bizarre, and a calm, serene Brandywine landscape by Andrew Wyeth which she thought was wonderfully beautiful.

Both the Newlands, particularly John, were very impressed that she could identify the painter and subject. He was watching Mathilda intently, aware that he was seeing his daughter, his flesh and blood, in her ancestral home.

"How do you know about Andrew Wyeth?" he asked.

"Read about it in a book," said Mathilda simply. She peered at the old photographs in antique frames that crowded the mantelpiece. "Who are these people?"

"These are old pictures of Grandfather," said John, as if introducing her to her own relatives. "He's standing in front of this house. See? Recognize the porch? That's my father next to him."

"Where are you?"

"I wasn't born yet."

"Oh," she said, turning away. To Mathilda these were just old pictures of people she didn't know and never would. Far more interesting, was the lavishly illustrated book on horses that sat on the coffee table. She turned the pages reverently, gazing on the beautiful old lithographs.

"Horses," she said solemnly. "They're *so* beautiful."

"Mathilda, would you like to see some real horses?" asked John Newland.

Mathilda nodded. "Yes, sir. If it wouldn't be too much trouble."

"No trouble," said Newland. "What would a guided tour be without a visit to the stables?"

Just then the Newland's elderly butler entered the room. He looked just as stuffy as in her father's impersonation. "Tea, suh?" he asked in his plummy accent.

"No thank you, Lewis. We were just going to show our guest the horses."

Lewis bowed slightly. "Very good, suh."

Mathilda did her best to stifle her laughter, but she giggled all the way to the stables.

One of the grooms was currycombing a polo

pony in the stable yard when they arrived. The man stepped back respectfully, holding the animal's bridle.

"Put a saddle on her," John Newland ordered.

"Yes, sir," said the groom, retreating into the tack room to get a saddle.

Mathilda stroked the horse's muzzle while the saddle was placed on the animal's back, the groom cinching the girth strap tight.

"Ever gotten up on a horse, Mathilda?"

"No, sir," she said.

"I'll show you. Take the reins in your left hand and put your left foot in the stirrup. . . ."

Mathilda did as she was told, leaning on the horse's flank for support. "Like this?"

"That's right. Now bend your right leg at the knee." John Newland reached down and took hold of her leg and boosted her into the saddle. "See. Nothing to it."

Mathilda was perched in the saddle, slightly breathless, and thrilled to discover that there was no view in the world quite as marvelous as the one from the back of a horse.

"Here, hold on, and I'll walk you around." John took the bridle and walked the horse across the yard, Mathilda hanging on to the pommel of the saddle.

Nancy couldn't help but notice that the little girl seemed to make her husband come alive. Much as he might pretend that children did not interest him, she could tell that he was enchanted with Mathilda, delighted to see that she shared his passion for horses.

"You look good up there, Mathilda," said Nancy.

John Newland walked a little faster and the horse broke into a trot.

"Here, take the reins. Sit up straight, heels down in the stirrups. . . . That's right." Mathilda was unsteady in the saddle, but she was eager to take control of the horse trotting around the yard.

"There you go!" said John. "It's Annie Oakley! The fastest gal on a horse this town has ever seen!"

Michael emerged from the house, wiping his hands on a rag. "All done, Mrs. Newland," he said.

"Dad, look!"

"You look great, honey."

John Newland took Michael aside. "Michael, Mathilda seems to have a passion for horses. Little girls always do, I guess. I had thought of inviting her up here so we could give her some lessons, but I thought I'd better clear it with you first. What do you think?"

Michael looked over his shoulder watching his daughter clip-clop around the stable yard. "I think she would love that," he said with a smile. "Actually, I *know* she would."

John Newland nodded. "Good. Do you mind if I tell her?"

"Be my guest," said Michael. "And thank you, Mr. Newland. This isn't the first time you've helped her. I hope it won't be too much trouble for you."

"Think nothing of it," said Newland. "It's no

trouble at all. We have a lot of horses and they all need exercise. I'll give her the lessons myself." He did not mention that his own father had taught him how to ride.

Mathilda almost jumped for joy when John Newland told her the news. All three adults were delighted to see how happy the little girl was. Michael was grateful that the Newlands were giving his daughter something he could not have afforded himself. But no one could have known that this apparently innocent gesture would change everything.

16

John and Nancy Newland both felt curiously letdown after the McCanns departed. The house seemed empty without the little girl, the echo of her laughter, and her happiness a distant memory. The intensity of her husband's delight in Mathilda moved and saddened Nancy.

"I'm sorry," Nancy said softly, as they walked back to the house.

"Sorry for what?"

"I'm sorry that I couldn't give you what you wanted. It's my fault."

John Newland was silent and could not bring himself to meet his wife's earnest gaze.

Nancy pressed on, heedless of how painful the conversation was to both of them. "You look at her and I can see how you feel. And I wish I could have given you this."

"It's all done, Nancy," said John Newland quietly. "It's all done."

"No. . . . No, it's not," she insisted. "We could have had a family. Why wouldn't you adopt?"

John turned away brusquely. "This is not something I choose to discuss."

"Don't turn your back on me, John, please."

"Nancy, we've been through this a hundred times and I—"

"Adopted children become your own children," said Nancy passionately. "Look at Michael McCann! He's a single man and he doesn't have half our resources and the state gave him custody. He and his daughter—that's right, *his* daughter—are happy and content."

"Michael McCann has her because of me," he said.

Nancy nodded. "I know. You helped him get custody of her. Why you don't help yourself, I don't understand. I'll never understand, I guess."

"That's not what I mean." He turned back, this time staring deep into her eyes. "That's not what I mean at all. He has her *because* of me."

"I don't understand," said Nancy with a shake of her head. "What are you saying to me?"

John opened his mouth, but for a long time, he could not speak. He was never at a loss for words, but this was the first time he had ever tried to talk about this with anyone.

But the stricken look on his face spoke volumes. Suddenly, Nancy understood.

"Are you saying that Mathilda is your daughter?"

"I thought I could be strong," John whispered. "But having her in the house today . . ." He shrugged, unable to put his emotions into words. "The woman who was found in the snow—Marsha. She was the mother. . . ." He sighed heavily. Facing the long buried truth did not come easy.

Nancy shook her head and stared at the ground, as if concentrating, adding up the numbers in her head, putting together the whole complicated sum.

"I thought it was strange," she said. "It seemed strange that you, usually so indifferent to children seemed so close to Mathilda. But now I understand. . . . It wasn't strange at all." She sounded sad and drained, as if resigned to her sorrow.

"I hope you won't leave me over this, Nancy," he said. "I know I should have told you a long time ago. . . ."

"There were times when I wanted to leave," she said, with a weak smile. "But this is not one of them."

"I didn't realize you were unhappy," he said. "I guess I should have been paying more attention."

"It wasn't that. . . . After we lost the child, I thought I was bringing you too much pain. But then I thought if you married someone else, they might be able to give you children. . . . But they might bring you pain in another way. Why did you keep this secret for so long?"

"If I had told anyone back then, I would have been ruined politically. I would never have gotten the party to back me. If I had told you, I don't think you would have stayed." He smiled ruefully and shook his head. "Either way, I guess I was just being selfish. Always looking out for old number one, that's me, you know."

"If you had taken her, she would have known me as her mother and you would have been happier with me. Our life would have been more like what we thought it would be."

John nodded. "I see it now, of course. But it's ten years too late." Two terms as a congressman, too many meetings with people like Strong and Hamilton had taken the gilt off being in politics. "I chose the wrong path. I went through the wrong door."

"It's not too late, John." Nancy's voice was filled with resolve. "You are her natural father. *You* are her father. And she deserves to be your daughter."

Mathilda had grown out of her nightly reading lessons—but Michael hadn't. After the excitement of the day, he couldn't think of a better way to calm down than with a good book. He selected one of his favorites from his library.

"Want me to read *Charlotte's Web*?" he asked Mathilda.

"Sure, go ahead. . . ." Then the penny dropped. "Oh, you want to read it to *me*."

"That's the idea."

Mathilda gave an anything-to-oblige sort of shrug and sat down on the sofa next to her father. She had heard the story a hundred times before, of course, so she didn't really have to follow very closely. As Michael read, Mathilda's mind swam with dreams—not of Charlotte the spider and her pal, Wilbur, the pig, but of the Newland's stables and their magnificent horses.

By the time Michael got to the end of the story, he was in tears, and Mathilda had imagined that she had won the Kentucky Derby and had become the greatest show jumper in the history of the sport. It took her a moment or two to realize that her father was deeply moved by Charlotte's untimely demise.

"There, there, Dad," she said, patting his knee. "It'll be okay. It's just a story, you know."

Michael nodded and wiped away his tears. "I know. I'm sorry, it's just so beautiful. . . ."

"You'll get over it, Dad," she said. The phone was ringing and she dove for it. "Hello. Hi, Mrs. Newland. . . ." She listened for a moment. "Just a minute, I have to ask my Dad." She put her hand over the receiver. "Mrs. Newland wants to know if I want to go on a horseback ride on Saturday. It's okay, isn't it?"

"Sure," said Michael.

Mathilda grinned as she got back on the phone. "He says that would be fine, Mrs. Newland. Thank you very much." She hung up and threw her arms around her father's neck. "The Newlands are so great, aren't they, Dad?"

"Yeah, great. Just great."

And yet something unnerved him about all this, something he couldn't quite put his finger on. It was no secret that the Newlands wanted but could not have children. It would be only natural for them to take an interest in his daughter—after all, they had been keeping an eye on her since she had come to Burrows. He tried to quell his suspicious thoughts, telling himself to just be thankful that the Newlands were making his daughter so happy.

And yet, something still bothered him. . . .

17

Before long, Mathilda was visiting the Newlands three and four times a week, and under John's expert tutelage, she quickly mastered the basics of riding. In addition, the grooms were instructing her in how to care for the animals, as if one day she would have the run of the stables as the lady of the great house.

But Mathilda was learning more than horsemanship. Nancy gave a feminine side to her childhood, teaching her things that Michael didn't know, things that never occurred to him that she *should* know. Michael had done a good job of raising his daughter, but she was a little rough around the edges when it came to doing her hair, or dressing with anything approaching flair. Nancy took over in that department, braiding the little girl's hair, quietly supplementing her wardrobe with a few discreet purchases, and allowing her to experiment with her own makeup, lipstick, and perfumes.

The Newlands' generosity was not born from an altruistic desire to assist one of their less fortunate tenants, nor was it a surreptitious attempt to assuage the guilt that John Newland felt—a bid to make up for all the years of neglect and indifference. The riding lessons, the presents, the devoted attention—all of these things were part of a subtle campaign to regain Mathilda, to bring her back into the Newland family, where, they felt, she rightfully belonged.

Randy Keating was the only person let in on the secret. As the Newlands' personal attorney, he had been put to work researching the legal rights of natural parents vis-à-vis those of adoptive ones. His inquiries were proceeding slowly, but in the meantime he had evolved a campaign to win Mathilda over. Once John and Nancy Newland had captured her heart, then winning her by the law would be a breeze.

"What you're doing is very good," Keating told Nancy. "Keep asking her over here as much as possible. Let her get used to first class."

Nancy was not convinced. "I know Mathilda. It will take more than riding lessons and a dab of Chanel to get her used to the idea of living here."

"It's not the kid I'm worried about. It's the battle for public opinion that concerns me."

"I don't understand."

"Nancy," said Keating, "you know that eventually this is going to go to court, and I have to tell you that right now, you and John do not look good. Here you are, the rich people up on the hill taking a little girl away from the man who took her in when no one else wanted her. The man who raised her, the man who struggled and saved, and blah-blah-blah. If I didn't know you, I would hate you myself."

Nancy closed her eyes, as if a pain had shot through her. "I would hate to have people think—"

"Well, that's what they would think right now if we told them about it." Keating smiled, his eyes full of cunning. "On the other hand, with a little positive spin we'll have every Joe six-pack in town eating out of our hand. . . ."

"I don't understand."

"It's simple. They all want to win the lottery. Well, we have to make them see that this kid has. Overnight she goes from being a beggar to being a princess. They'll eat it up. We'll even have *McCann* believing that she'll have a better life with you than she would with the old woodcutter who lives in a lean-to in the forest."

"He's a furniture maker."

"Whatever," said Keating dismissively.

"And he has a nice little house. I've seen it myself."

Keating grinned. "Is it as nice as this?"

"No . . ." Nancy sighed. "So our money may finally have a use."

"Oh yeah," said Keating with a self-satisfied smirk. "*Finally*."

John Newland was waiting for Mathilda the next time she came for a riding lesson.

"Hi, Mathilda."

"Hi, Mr. Newland," she said, flashing him her brightest smile.

"Ready to ride?" he asked.

"Always!"

"Good. Look." The groom had led three horses out of the stable instead of the usual two.

"Which of these do you like best?" John Newland asked, nodding toward the three mounts.

It hadn't taken Mathilda very long to become something of a judge of horseflesh. "I think the second one," she said. "She's strong *and* pretty."

"Good choice. I want you to have her."

Mathilda blinked. "Huh?"

"She's yours."

The girl could hardly believe her ears. "Mine? Really? Holy smokes!"

"You could keep her up here. Ride her any time you feel like it."

"I don't know what to say."

"You *could* give her a name."

Mathilda was completely flabbergasted, dazzled by the generosity of her new friend. "Holy *smokes*."

"That's the name?"

"No. . . no . . . I'd have to do some research, but the name Sparkle immediately comes to mind."

John Newland laughed. "Listen, you can call her Flipper if you want to. She's yours."

The full weight of Newland's words were just beginning to sink in. It was every little girl's dream come true. "Thank you. *Thank you*!"

John Newland put his arm around Mathilda's shoulders and he spoke quietly. "Look, I think we should keep this between the two of us, just for a little while."

"How come?"

"Just our little secret, that's all."

But that wasn't good enough for Mathilda. "Why?"

John Newland shrugged. "Okay, you *could* tell your dad if you want, but he might not like it. Parents can be funny about something like this."

"Really?"

"Think about it. Now, let's get into the saddle. We'll ride down by Stone Lake, then we'll get back to the house in time for tea and cakes."

"Tea?"

John Newland laughed out loud. "Absolutely."

Mathilda rode until her legs hurt, then gorged herself on tea and cakes. Happy and sated, she rode her bike home. Her father was waiting for her with a plate of her favorite snack.

"Just in time for some nachos," he said, proffering a plate of corn chips covered with a mound of hot, oily cheese fresh from the microwave. The nachos suffered by comparison to the light and delicate tea cakes served by the Newlands' butler.

"I'm full," Mathilda said. She escaped to her room, hoping that her father wasn't going to press the issue.

Her hopes were dashed. No sooner had she flung herself on her bed then Michael put his head around the door.

"I think we should talk," he said solemnly.

"We should? Already, I don't like it."

Michael sat down on the edge of the bed. "I just think that maybe you shouldn't go up to the Newlands' house so much."

"Why?" Mathilda looked sharply at her father. She didn't like the sound of this at all—and she could see that Mr. Newland had done the right thing in making her horse a little secret just between the two of them. Pure instinct told her that her dad would not appreciate her receiving such an extravagant gift. John Newland had hinted that this would happen—and now she admired him all the more.

"You . . . you live here. And it's possible to overstay your welcome."

"But they invite me," Mathilda insisted. "Why would they invite me if they didn't want me to be there?"

"I think it's too much," he said.

"Well, I'm going," she said obstinately.

"Not so much, not so often."

"I want to go!" she yelled.

"Well, sometimes you can't have everything you want," he said gruffly, laying down the law for once. "You can't be greedy about everything."

"Huh, look who's talking," said Mathilda with a scornful snort.

"What does that mean?"

"Look who's talking about being greedy," she said triumphantly. "You of all people!"

"What do you *mean*?"

"They told me at school that you were a miser,

that you loved money! You loved it so much you kept it at home so you could look at it! And that's why it was stolen, because you wouldn't put it in a bank like everybody else!"

Michael was dumbfounded that the kids at school were gossiping about him, amazed that they even knew of what had happened to him all those years ago. It was obvious to him that their parents had told them, but he couldn't imagine why they would be bother, or why a bunch of third graders would be interested.

In spite of being taken aback by his daughter's cruel words, he stuck to his guns. "You listen to me, young lady," he said, real anger seizing him. "I say you are not going to the Newland house anymore and that's final!"

"Yes, I am!" she screamed, red in the face now. "I'll do what I want!"

"You'll do what I tell you and I'm telling you that you are not going there anymore!"

"Yes, I am! Yes, I am!"

Michael shook his head slowly and walked out of the room, closing the door firmly behind him. He was trembling with anger, annoyed at himself for losing his temper and furious at John and Nancy Newland for driving this sharp wedge between father and daughter.

The next few days brought the first real cold war between Michael and Mathilda. He was surprised—he had assumed that Mathilda would calm down and be her usual loving self again. But the Newlands had quite a hold on her and she gave him the silent treatment. She said hardly a word to him at breakfast and wouldn't even look at him when he and April Simon showed up at her gymnastics demonstration on Friday afternoon.

At best, Mathilda was only a mediocre gymnast, but of course, Michael, who could not take his eyes off her, saw nothing short of genius in everything his daughter attempted.

"She is definitely good," he said, as Mathilda managed to pull off a ragged back flip.

"She's fine," said April Simon.

"Fine? Only fine?"

"Good," said April quickly. "She's good."

"If she's not doing it perfectly, it's because she's in a bad mood," said Michael.

"Bad mood? Mathilda is *never* in a bad mood."

"She hates me right now," Michael explained, "but she'll get over it."

Mrs. Simon nodded knowingly, very much the older, wiser, more experienced parent. "Oh yeah, in five or six years she could be over it. . . . you know, with therapy, and Prozac shaped like the Flintstones. She doesn't mean it."

"Right," said Michael. "They don't mean it and then, when you're not looking, they shoot you."

"Eeew," said April disgusted. "I don't want to think about it."

Mathilda pulled off another back flip, much better this time. Michael clapped and hooted, but she wouldn't so much as glance in his direction. He jabbed April sharply in the ribs.

"See that guy over there?" He pointed to a well-dressed man who had just come into the gymnasium. The double-breasted suit he wore was sharp, and he carried an expensive briefcase. It was plain that he wasn't from Burrows or any of the other rural villages in the area.

"Yes, what about him?"

"I think he's a scout."

"A scout?"

"A scout from the United States Olympic Team. I'll bet he's here to check out Mathilda."

"Oh, *undoubtedly*."

"You laugh," Michael whispered, "but he's headed this way."

"That your daughter?" the man in the suit asked Michael. April wondered if all of the scouts for the U.S. Olympic Team had such shifty eyes.

"Quite a talent isn't she?" said Michael.

The guy did not even crack a smile. "You are Michael McCann, right?"

Michael nodded. "That's right. I'm her father and I am also her agent."

"Nice," said the man sourly. He reached into his briefcase and thrust a thick sheaf of official-looking papers into Michael's hands.

"What's this?"

"You are served." The man in the suit turned to leave. "If I were you, I'd get a lawyer."

"A lawyer?" Then he looked at the papers. With a sickening sense of déjà vu, it hit him. Someone else was claiming his child.

18

We should definitely count on drumming up some sympathy," Nancy said. "Cal Mosley can help. He's sure to give you favorable coverage in the newspaper. He's always been on your side." She thought for a moment. "We should get him to play up the angle that you were the victim, back then, of an overly strict political climate."

"That's funny," said John Newland. "I thought I was a victim of my own greed and ambition."

"Don't make jokes like that," said Nancy sharply.

Nancy approached the campaign to gain custody of Mathilda the way a general plans for a war. She considered every angle, every tactic; she evaluated her foes, charting their strengths and weaknesses; and she assembled her allies and worked to keep them in line.

It was as though she was compensating for her physical inability to give her husband a child and was now working overtime to see that he was reunited with his own flesh and blood. She never thought about Mathilda's biological mother, as if the legal crusade was her own act of motherhood, her own way of bestowing life on a child.

John Newland took his wife's hand in his. "We'll win," he said. "And it will be your victory."

"There's quite a way to go," she said, "before we break out the champagne."

Neither of them was particularly surprised to hear Michael McCann's old truck laboring up their driveway and coming to a halt with a screech of brakes in front of the house.

A moment later he burst into the study, the old butler trailing breathlessly in his wake.

"You're not getting her!" Michael yelled. "Do you hear me? You're not getting my little girl."

"I'm terribly sorry, Mr. Newland," said the butler. "I—this gentleman—should I call the police?"

John Newland shook his head. "No. It's all right, Lewis. We can deal with it."

"There's nothing to deal with," Michael shouted. "She's my daughter and that's that."

"I would think you would want what is good for her," said Nancy hotly. "Think of the child instead of yourself."

Michael spoke as if his words were carved in stone. "You are not getting her."

"But she's not yours, McCann," said John Newland firmly. "She's not yours."

"The hell she isn't!"

"Michael, she is my child. I am her biological father and that is profoundly unchangeable. I just want to be with my daughter. Is that so hard to understand?"

"If you love her so much, then why did you turn your back on her ten years ago? She would have died in the snow if it hadn't been for me." Michael's voice sounded like thunder and he spoke with all the passion of a righteous man. "Or she would have been imprisoned in an orphanage or shipped off, shuttled from foster home to foster home. Don't tell *me* about fatherhood, Newland. You don't know the first thing about it."

Suddenly it seemed to John Newland as if excuses about the harsh political climate seemed flimsy and feeble, hardly likely to stand in the face of a man who had sacrificed everything to raise a child no one had wanted.

But as Michael turned to storm from the house, it was Nancy who launched the counterattack. She flew after him, her features twisted in rage, ugly in her anger. Michael marched through the house and down the front step towards his truck. Nancy was right behind him.

"Michael, it's inevitable. Do you hear me? Inevitable!" she snarled. "You can fight it or not, but she's going to end up here. Given time, there is no way she would not prefer her real father, and this family."

Michael turned on her and stared her down. "It doesn't seem to bother you too much, destroying lives like this. . . . You might want her now, but it's me she's been calling daddy ever since she could say the word."

Nancy's anger intensified. "Listen—" Then

she stopped. Mathilda was standing just outside the front door, holding her bike. She stared intently at the two adults. Nancy did her best to compose herself, to conceal her anger.

"Hello, Mathilda."

"Hello, ma'am . . . Is it true that Mr. Newland is my real father?"

Nancy nodded and avoided Michael's furious gaze. "Yes, dear, he is."

"My biological father," said Mathilda, as if double-checking her facts.

"Well, yes . . ." Nancy Newland managed a bright smile. "Isn't that great news? Wouldn't you like to come and live here with us?"

Mathilda glanced at her father and then looked away, her eyes downcast. "I don't know. I don't know what I'm supposed to say to you." She backed away from them, then rode off on her bike.

Michael looked at John. "When you turn a gift away from your door," he said solemnly, "it goes to the one who takes it in."

By the time he got home, Michael's anger had subsided, leaving him tired and drained. He found it hard to believe that this ordinary, commonplace day had turned into a nightmare from which there seemed to be no escape. The door to Mathilda's room was shut, but he could hear her crying. He wanted to go to her immediately, but he hung back, waiting until she called to him.

Michael entered the room gingerly. There were still tears in her eyes, but now she was deep in thought, as if slowly working out a huge and complicated equation in her head.

When she did speak, it was to ask the one of the questions that Michael had been dreading for a decade. "Dad . . ." she asked in a very small voice, "where was my mother buried?"

Somewhere in the back of his mind, Michael knew that this day would come, that one day he would have to face questions to which he had no answers.

"We don't really know," he said slowly. "We never knew where she was taken."

"Why not?"

"I was afraid," Michael said. "I was afraid they might find relatives. Or the vanished father, or someone who would take you away from me. You have to understand me, Mathilda, you have to understand what it was like. I was alone."

Mathilda took her father's hand. "One day I would like to know where she is."

Michael nodded. "I can work on it. Mrs. Simon can find anything on her computer." Then he remembered something. "Uh, just a minute . . ." From a small wooden box on his tool bench, he took the silver charm bracelet he had found in the snow all those years before.

"This was your mother's," he said, placing the chain in her hand. "You should have it."

Mathilda examined the little bauble closely, turning it over in her hands. The faintest look of recognition played across her serious features. It seemed that it wasn't the object itself that she remembered, but the muted clink of the silver links. "Thank you," she said finally. She put the bracelet on and held her wrist out to admire it.

"It's you and her, isn't it . . . ? I mean, it's just you and her. You're my parents. You and Mom. Not the Newlands. You and her."

The conversation was straying dangerously close to the subject of sex, a topic that Michael had never been particularly comfortable with.

"I'll make you a drink," he said, nervously, turning toward the kitchen.

"A drink!"

"Uh . . . a juice, uh, drink." Then he took a deep breath. It was better to face these things headon, he decided. "Look . . . do you know what it means that he's your real dad?" Michael squirmed uneasily. "I mean, do you *know* how babies are made? I mean to say, do you know that—"

Mathilda rescued her father from his embarrassment, trying not to laugh, but failing to supress a smile. "Oh, come on, Dad. I know what's what."

"Good," said Michael, considerably relieved. It was one less thing he had to worry about and just then, he had plenty.

19

The story hit the papers coast to coast, for there was nothing that the public liked more than a juicy child-custody battle. The matter of *Newland v. McCann,* as the legal system styled it, had more than enough sensational details to quicken the pulse of the most jaded tabloid editor.

Any truly great scandal has two elements: sex and money. The Newland affair had both. The financial angle was the stuff of dreams: the little girl, born a pauper, now the lone heir to an old and very great fortune. The sexual side of things was no less exciting: the sexual secrets of a handsome congressman brought to light so that he might claim his daughter. No wonder, editors and publishers, cursed with a slow news season, were blessing the name of John Newland.

As expected, Cal Mosely threw the support of his own paper behind John Newland big-time. There was a banner, six-point headline on page one: GIVE ME BACK MY DAUGHTER!, along with a heartrending photograph of John Newland. Gone was the cool, self-assured, handsome politician.

In his place was a stricken, neglected father, his head in his hands, his face grave and drawn.

Nancy thought it was a perfect opening shot. "It couldn't have been any better if you had written it yourself."

John Newland smirked. "I did write it."

Nancy smiled as she paged through the newspaper. On page five there was a picture of Michael McCann. It hadn't been as carefully staged as John's had been. Rather, the photographer had snapped Michael near his house, stalking him like a wild animal. Michael had seen the photographer at the last minute and had waved him off angrily. The shutter clicked, catching Michael looking sullen and glowering, a forest in the background—it looked as if Michael McCann was a bad-tempered troll from deep in the woods.

"You'll have the whole town on your side in no time," she said. "And public opinion couldn't be more important."

"I know that," John Newland said. "I'm in politics, don't forget." He smiled at his wife. "As for getting the whole town on my side, you're overlooking one person who is never on my side. It would kill him."

"Who?"

"Jerry Bryce, of course."

Nancy laughed quietly. "I'd say we could handle Jerry Bryce, wouldn't you?"

Bryce always knew that he would get his chance to take on John Newland and now the eagerly awaited day had finally dawned. He knew that Michael McCann would come to him for help—there were two practicing lawyers in Burrows. Jerry Bryce was one, the other was Randy Keating. Bright and early Monday morning, Michael McCann came calling. Talking to a lawyer made him most uncomfortable. The only time he had needed one before was to arrange for his divorce from Elaine. Not surprisingly, he associated the legal profession with pain and public humiliation.

He found Bryce itching for the fight. "The Newlands have hired Randy Keating to represent them."

"Do you know him?"

Bryce nodded. "He's an old rival of mine, but I'll try to keep that out of it. He cheats at polo, too, and he'll cheat at this."

"Polo?"

"Forget about it." He studied the summons that Michael had given him. "The first thing they'll do is bring up the money issue. They've got a lot—you haven't. At least, I assume you haven't."

"No," said Michael miserably. "If they bring up the money, then I'm sunk."

Bryce shook his head impatiently. "No. It's not like that. If they bring up money, then they're fools. The courts don't consider money in these cases, or at least, they aren't supposed to."

Michael cleared his throat. "As regards money . . ." He had no idea what this was going to cost him. He could only assume it would cost somewhere in the region of a small fortune.

Bryce waved him off. "I want you to know you'll have me for nothing. I enjoy the competition."

Michael was moved and felt a little better to think that there was *someone* on his side. "Thank you," he said. "I appreciate that. I'll try and pay you one day."

"Yeah, well, don't worry about it," said Bryce. "First things first. I hope you understand that you are up against a well-connected, politically astute couple. Nancy and John Newland are highly motivated—not to mention highly rich."

"Yes," said Michael stoutly. "But I have something they *don't* have."

Jerry leaned back in his desk chair and eyed Michael curiously. "And what would that be?"

"I am right," said Michael simply.

Jerry Bryce smiled ruefully and shook his head, trying to let Michael down easily. "Right only mattered to our forefathers," he said. "We have to have a little more than that."

Mathilda was waiting for him when he returned from Jerry Bryce's office, her baleful gaze firing a dozen questions at him all at once.

"What?" he asked irritably. "What?"

"I'm not going to have to move up there, am I?" The little girl advanced a step. "I mean, this *is* home, isn't it?"

"Of course you don't have to move. And, *of course,* this is home."

"You're sure?"

"Well . . ." He hated to admit that the subject

had not really come up. He assumed that she would stay with him while the matter was *sub judice*. As for the future, he couldn't really say.

Mathilda sensed her father's indecision. She folded her arms across her chest. "Well, what the *hell* am I going to do if I have to go and live up there?"

Michael wasn't sure he could believe what he had heard her say. "Did you say 'hell?' "

Mathilda nodded vigorously. "You bet I did."

"Well, don't say it."

"I can use it if I want," said Mathilda defiantly. "I can say anything I want. I can say *shit* if I want—"

"Mathilda," Michael cautioned ominously.

But she was beginning to break down, the upsetting events of the last few days beginning to overwhelm her. Tears were streaming down her cheeks and her voice sounded high and tight.

"I don't have to say everything you want me to say. I don't have to do everything you tell me to. I don't have to—I don't—" She ran from the room and threw herself on her bed, hugging her pillow, crying as if she felt the pain in her own soul.

Michael followed her and took her in his arms. "It's okay," he said, smoothing her hair. "It's all right. All right. Don't cry, honey. . . . It's all right. . . ."

Mathilda turned her tearstained face up to his. "Daddy . . . this is really happening. Good grief."

"I know," said Michael. "I know. But we'll

get through it. There's nothing to worry about. I won't let them take you from me. Ever."

"Promise?"

"Promise." Michael held her until she fell asleep, all the while praying that this was one promise he could keep.

Once the newspapers broke the story of John Newland's campaign to regain custody of his daughter, the tabloid television shows pounced on Burrows, carpeting the little town with camera crews, relay trucks, and self-important correspondents who pursued the hapless residents of the town, prying and meddling, butting in where they weren't wanted.

Mathilda could not quite believe that *she* was news, but she was and it took some getting used to. Once the trial began though, Michael and Mathilda forgot that they were in the middle of a media carnival and concentrated on the fact that they were locked in a life and death struggle with the Newlands.

This was not to be a jury trial. Bryce couldn't make up his mind if this helped or hindered their cause. Juries could do strange things, they were capable of ignoring the most basic points of law and focusing on something obscure, something dim and indefinite that neither attorney had paid much attention to.

On the other hand, the lawyers would have to convince Judge Marcus alone of the validity of their arguments. Having Marcus on the bench delighted Randy Keating, but it did not please

Bryce. He knew that the judge was a fair man, but he also knew that he was a close friend of John Newland. But Judge Marcus was the only sitting jurist in the county, so Bryce was stuck with him. He hoped that the judge would not allow personal friendships to influence his ruling.

All of the players were in place, and the courtroom was packed when Randy Keating called his first witness, Mrs. Latham, the principal of Mathilda's school.

She took the oath and sat in the witness box, awaiting the first question. She did not look particularly comfortable at having been dragged into this, and she looked even more ill at ease when Keating began circling around the witness box like a shark who smelled blood in the water.

"Mrs. Latham, you are currently are the principal and teacher at the school . . . Mathilda Newland's school, are you not?"

"Yes," said Mrs. Latham.

Mathilda couldn't quite believe what she had heard. "Mathilda Newland?" she whispered in April Simon's ear. "Who is this Mathilda Newland?"

"Don't worry," April hissed back. "They're just trying to get your goat."

"Congratulations are in order," harrumphed Mathilda. "They did."

Randy Keating pressed a little harder. "And speaking as a teacher, Mrs. Latham, do you think Mathilda Newland has the ability to do well in college?"

"She's a very bright girl," said Mrs. Latham. "I can imagine her doing well, yes."

"And do you think this child has the potential to attend a prestigious college? An Ivy League school. Harvard, say? Or Yale?"

"It's a little early to tell," said Mrs. Latham. "She's only a little girl."

"But reflect for a moment," said Randy Keating. "You've seen a lot of students pass through your care over the years. Some of them have gone on to renowned schools. They must have something in common with Mathilda Newland."

Mrs. Latham nodded. "Mathilda has unlimited potential. She could accomplish great things."

Keating nodded. "Including going to Harvard?"

"Indeed."

The lawyer followed up quickly. "Do you know what it costs to attend Harvard or Yale?"

Mrs. Latham shrugged. "I don't know . . . I'm sure it is not cheap."

Randy Keating smiled his most charming smile. "Thank you Mrs. Latham. That will be all."

Mrs. Latham looked slightly confused. "That's it?"

"That's it."

There was a low rumble of disappointment from the spectators as Mrs. Latham left the witness stand. They had been expecting fireworks and all they got were a couple of obscure questions about the cost of going to college in a faraway, Northern state. Not very entertaining.

However, the next witness promised to be a lot

more fun. "The court calls Mrs. April Simon," the bailiff called out.

Before going to the stand, April whispered in Mathilda's ear. "Wait till he gets me up there. Keating thinks he's getting little Aunt Mildred with an antique shop. What he's getting is Aunt Attila the Hun."

"Go get 'em," said Mathilda.

Mrs. Simon placed her right hand on the Bible and raised her left. "Do you solemnly swear to tell the truth, the whole truth and nothing but the truth, so help you God?"

"You bet your boots," said April

Keating went right for the jugular. "You like Mr. McCann, don't you?" he asked bluntly.

"Well . . . yes."

"He is unmarried and you are unmarried."

"That is correct."

"And you've known him for how long?"

"Ten years or so," said Mrs. Simon. "About ten years, I guess."

"Have you ever had sexual relations with Mr. McCann?" Keating asked.

The crowd murmured again. The term "sexual relations" wasn't mentioned in polite society in rural Virginia.

Mrs. Simon flushed red. "Whatever we have done, we have done in private until you opened your big mouth. We have always been sensitive to Mathilda, and other than that, I'd like to say it's none of your business."

"I apologize," said Keating with a smirk.

"You should."

"And how would you characterize Mr. McCann? As a father, I mean."

"He's a great father," said Mrs. Simon resolutely. "He's caring, he thinks of nothing but that child. Any child would be lucky to have a father like that. . . ."

"Uh-huh," said Keating. He knew that the longer he let her talk, the more likely she was to make a mistake. Witnesses always wanted to hit a home run—they never realized that the less you said, the more you helped your own side.

"He teaches her at home, he looks out for his interests. He's marvelous. . . . He's very unconventional."

Randy Keating saw his opening and pounced. "Unconventional? Unconventional how?"

"I beg your pardon?"

"You said that Mr. McCann was unconventional with Mathilda Newland. How is he unconventional?"

Mrs. Simon felt a sinking feeling, a vague awareness that she was about to step into a trap. But she couldn't help herself—or Michael McCann. "Well, when Mathilda was just a toddler, in order to keep an eye on her, he used to tie her up with a red ribbon." In spite of herself, Mrs. Simon laughed. "We all thought it was hilarious."

"Tie her up?" said Keating sharply. "*Tie* her up?"

She shifted uncomfortably on the hard seat. "Well . . . not tie her up, exactly. He'd just tie her to a table leg or something like that. Just so he could keep an eye on her."

"I see," said Keating skeptically. "Uh-huh. He would tie her to a table leg. Could the ribbon have become entangled around her neck at all?"

"No," said Mrs. Simon quickly. "It was tied around her ankle."

"But children are active little creatures, aren't they," Randy Keating countered. "They move around a lot and it could have become entangled. . . . Not exactly the latest in enlightened parenting is it, Mrs. Simon?"

"Well, no. But . . ."

Keating circled for another attack. "What else? Did he do other things that you considered unconventional?"

"Well," said April cautiously. "He educated her in his own way, like when she was learning to read, he told her not to read the school books, and instead would give her adult books."

"He wouldn't let her read the books that were assigned to her in school? Is that correct?"

"Well, it wasn't that exactly. I mean she didn't *want* to read them."

"So he allowed her to read her school books?"

"Well, it wasn't that so much. . . . It's—he—" April Simon did her best to get hold of her thoughts.

"But she did read adult books?"

"Right."

"Adult books?"

"Well, not *those* kind of adult books," she said flustered. April turned to the judge. "May I be excused?"

"I'm afraid that's up to Mr. Keating."

Randy Keating smiled. "Thank you, Mrs. Simon," he said. "That is all."

April Simon was so anxious to get off the stand, she almost ran back to her seat. "Oh boy," she whispered to Mathilda. "I really stank."

Judge Marcus cleared his throat. "Mrs. Simon, we're not quite done with you yet."

"Oh shit," she said. "Excuse me."

Jerry Bryce was on his feet. "I have no questions for this witness."

"I don't blame you," said Mrs. Simon. She hung her head, well aware that she had done much to damage her friend's cause.

20

It had been an emotional day for everyone, but as far as Mathilda was concerned, nothing had been settled, none of her questions answered. On impulse, she rode her bicycle up to the Newland mansion and boldly knocked on the door. John Newland answered in person, surprised, but delighted to see her.

"Can I talk to you?" Mathilda asked.

"I'd like nothing more," he said. "Let's take a stroll." Newland took her arm and walked her along the wide porch. "What's on your mind?"

"I just have one question. . . ."

"And that is?"

"Who are you?"

John Newland smiled. "That's about the best question anyone's thought to ask me during this whole thing, Mathilda. Who am I? I am your real father."

"My *real* father?"

"That's right. Not the best father—I know that. I'm not even as good as Michael McCann has been up to now, but I know I can be. I may have made a mistake I will regret my whole life, and that's why I'm fighting for you. I know you think I'm hateful, but that's a chance I have to take."

"But what about me?"

"This is all about you, Mathilda. If you do end up here, I know you'll be happy in time, because I know I'm a decent person . . . a decent person who has made some mistakes. That's all. Just like Michael. I want to make up for all those mistakes. I need that chance."

Mathilda nodded and stared at him. "What was my mother like?"

John Newland could hardly remember her, but he knew he had to say something. "She was . . . your mother loved you. Mathilda, can you see that I do, too? However this works out, I want you to know that."

But Mathilda refused to let Newland to change the subject. "How did you treat my mother?"

"I treated her as best I could." Lying came easily to him. "I never hurt her. I respected her. We just weren't made for each other, that's all. I liked her. She was a good person who was under the influence of drugs. You've heard how bad that can be."

"Yes," said Mathilda with a little nod.

"Do you ever think about us?" John Newland asked. "Do you ever think that you could live up here?"

Tears sprang into Mathilda's eyes. "Sometimes. I think about it sometimes."

Newland shrugged. "I guess that's about the best I can hope for. . . ."

Courthouse regulars expected fireworks on the second day of the hearing. They were not disappointed when Randy Keating called John Newland as his first witness.

Keating had done his homework and he started out with an exhibit that had required quite a bit of fancy legal footwork to obtain. He showed Newland a collection of a few pieces of paper, bureaucratic forms, yellowed and dog-eared.

"Mr. Newland, these are admittance forms from the maternity ward at County General Hospital, for a Miss Marsha Swanson. Would you read the signature at the bottom, just here?"

Mathilda was transfixed at hearing her mother's name spoken out loud like that. She repeated the words to herself, whispering them like a mantra.

"It says, Mr. Henry Swanson," said John Newland.

Keating turned and faced the audience. "And who is Mr. Henry Swanson?"

"I am," said Newland. "I mean, I signed this paper using a different name."

"That is your handwriting?"

"Yes it is."

"Mr. Newland, how did you come to be the natural father of this child?"

Newland's shoulders sagged and he closed his eyes for a moment, as if reliving a painful memory. "I was twenty-nine years old. I met a woman and started seeing her secretly."

"And why secretly?"

"She was underage," said John Newland matter-of-factly. "She was seventeen, almost eighteen. She became pregnant. . . ."

"And why didn't you tell anyone about this?"

Newland smiled ruefully. "My father was still alive. He was a very disapproving man. I was afraid to tell him."

"So what did you do?"

"All I could," he said earnestly. "I paid for all her hospital bills and saw to it that she was taken care of. I made an arrangement with the mother that I would give her money on a monthly basis and this would remain our secret."

"And she agreed?"

"Yes, she did."

"And *why* did she agree?"

"She was a drug addict," said John Newland softly. "She didn't care about anything else. I didn't marry her because she wouldn't have been a fit wife much less a mother."

Mathilda frowned at this. She had hardly known her mother, of course, but she didn't like to hear her run down in public like that.

"She was an unfit mother. . . ." said Keating. "What were you, Mr. Newland?"

"Me? I was young and stupid . . . and afraid."

Keating smiled benignly. "Looking back now, you see how foolish you were."

John Newland hung his head in shame. "Yes. I do."

"The mother was an addict, yet Mathilda was not born addicted to drugs or damaged in any way. Do you have any idea how that happened?"

"Yes, I do. During her pregnancy, I saw to it that the mother stayed clean, off drugs. That was the least I could do. It wasn't easy, but it was important to me." He had told so many lies by now that one more scarcely seemed to matter.

Keating nodded, sensing that his client had made a good impression. "I have no further questions, Your Honor."

"Mr. Bryce," said Judge Marcus, "your witness."

Bryce bounced to his feet and strode toward the witness stand, his eyes boring into Newland.

"The night that child walked into McCann's house, you were there, were you not?"

"No, I wasn't," said Newland quickly.

"I mean, you were around that night. You knew the child had been discovered."

"Yes. Yes, I was."

"And you knew who it was?"

"Yes."

"And yet you did nothing."

Now it was John Newland's turn to feel uncomfortable on the witness stand. He could see where Jerry Bryce was going with his line of questioning, and he was powerless to stop it.

"I felt the child was in . . ."

"Mr. Newland," said Bryce sharply. "Please just answer the question. You said nothing, am I right?"

"Yes," admitted Newland.

Bryce pressed his attack. "And by failing to claim your daughter at that moment, you neither asserted your parental rights nor fulfilled your parental responsibilities."

"Objection," shouted Keating. "This assumes facts not in evidence."

"Sustained," said Judge Marcus.

"I'll rephrase," said Keating. "You did not act as though you were the father, you did not comfort her or hold her or do any of the things a father might do."

"No."

"So at the time, your feelings toward your future wife and your career dictated your actions more than your feelings for your child. Is that correct?"

John looked helplessly at his counsel, begging Randy Keating to intervene, to get him off the hook—but there was nothing his attorney could do either.

"Is that correct, Mr. Newland?" demanded Bryce.

"Yes," said Newland. "But since then I have made sure that she was safe and in this community where I could watch over her and see that she was well taken care of."

"You're breaking our hearts," said Bryce coldly. "Why did you see the mother in secret?"

"Well, I would have thought that would be obvious," said John Newland.

"Obvious to you maybe. Why don't you tell us?"

John Newland could not escape the consequences of his own actions and his answer sounded cold, overweeningly proud. "Because she was not the kind of person one should be seen with. It would not have been appropriate for me to be seen with her."

Virtually everyone in the room was thinking the same thing, but Randy Bryce spoke the words out loud. "But appropriate to sleep with? She was appropriate for a little fling, because, hey, after all, what did it matter, right?"

"Objection! Argumentative."

"Sustained. Be careful, Mr. Bryce."

"Sorry, Your Honor." Bryce did not feel even slightly contrite, but he had to pretend. "You did not want to be seen with her because you were in politics?"

"Yes."

"Better to lie to the public."

"No!" John Newland shot back. "I made a mistake. I admit that."

"You admit it because you have to admit it," Bryce snapped. "You have to admit it so you can look like a man with a modicum of remorse."

"No," he protested. "She trapped me. I was young and afraid."

Bryce went for the throat now. "That was why you were paying her off, correct? To get this little embarrassment out of your life?"

John Newland was rattled now. His collar and tie felt tight, his throat constricted. "No . . . she was out of control. Addicts only care about themselves."

Mathilda could not take her eyes from John

Newland. She could not tell if he was telling the truth or merely putting on a skillful act, playing to the crowd, begging for sympathy. The fact that she couldn't tell disturbed her. Mathilda like things to be plain and up-front. In that moment she realized she couldn't love a man she couldn't trust.

21

Of all the people called to the witness stand that week, Mathilda was the only one really prepared to do battle with Randy Keating. She was full of fight and convinced that she was in the right. In addition, she alone carried no old baggage to the stand—rare was the ten-year-old who had skeletons in her closet. She also had an ace up her sleeve, or rather, in her pocket. It was a small jar of acrid smelling mentholatum, the disinfectant fumes never failed to bring tears to Mathilda's eyes.

Randy Keating knew that he had to be careful with child witnesses. They were volatile and one could never tell what they would say. The old lawyers' adage—never ask a question without knowing the answer—did not apply when you had a child on the stand.

"Hi, Mathilda," he said pleasantly, leaning on the rail that surrounded the witness chair.

"Hi," said Mathilda.

"How are you?"

"Not so good."

"How's your horse?"

If Mathilda was taken aback by the question, Michael, sitting at the defendant's table was flabbergasted. "Her what?" he gasped.

"He asked her how her horse is." Bryce was furiously making notes on a yellow legal pad.

"She doesn't *have* a horse."

"Guess again," muttered Bryce.

"I asked how your horse is doing," said Keating. "you know, your pony Sparkle, I think her name is."

"I don't know," said Mathilda. "We haven't been in touch."

"But you do own a horse."

Mathilda shrugged. "I guess."

"How did you come to own a fine little horse like Sparkle? She's a thoroughbred, I understand."

"Mr. Newland gave her to me," Mathilda mumbled.

"And you accepted her," said Keating. "In fact, you were happy to have her."

"Yes."

"Did you tell Mr. McCann that your father had given you a horse?"

Mathilda had once had a feeling that this would come back to haunt her. It turned out that she did have a skeleton in her closet after all. She shook her head slowly. "Nope."

Keating summed up. "So you might say that you had a special relationship with your real father that you were afraid to tell Mr. McCann."

"I wasn't afraid," Mathilda protested.

"But you didn't tell him about the horse that your real dad gave you?"

"No."

"That's all, said Keating. "Thank you, Mathilda."

Unlike Keating, Jerry Bryce had been looking forward to cross-examining Mathilda McCann. The little girl was a natural actress and she would make an excellent witness for her side.

"So, Mathilda," he asked casually. "How do you like being known as Mathilda Newland?"

"It's not me."

"What do you like to be called?"

"Mathilda McCann," she said stoutly.

"Why is that?"

"Because that's my father's name."

She was doing so well, Bryce wanted to kiss her. "Would you point to the man you think of as your father?"

Mathilda did not hesitate. She pointed to Michael and beamed at him. "There's Dad, right over there."

"Thank you, Mathilda," said Jerry Bryce. "What is Mr. Newland to you?"

"Well . . . I used to think of him as a nice man."

"And what do you think of him now?"

"He's the man who is trying to take me away from my father."

John Newland winced at her words. "We're getting slaughtered here," he whispered.

Keating put a steadying hand on Newland's

forearm. "Just so long as she doesn't cry. Tears would not be good."

The lawyer did not get his wish. Mathilda had decided to swing into the second phase of her attack. She managed to get a little of the mentholatum under each eye.

"How would you feel if you were separated from your father?"

Right on cue, tears welled in Mathilda's eyes. "I . . . I . . ."

"Uh-oh," whispered Keating.

Two fat tears rolled down Mathilda's cheeks. "I could never be separated from him. . . . Never. . . . He's the one who's taken care of me, he's the one who inspired me." She sniffed deeply, wiped her eyes, adding a little more mentholatum. "Now as I enter the years of womanhood, I'll need his guidance more than ever. I couldn't be anything without my loving daddy."

Mathilda wasn't the only one in the courtroom who had tears in her eyes. Even Judge Marcus wiped at his eyes.

"Daddy?" said Mathilda holding out her arms. Michael was out of his seat like a shot, running to his little girl and taking her in his arms.

Jerry Bryce listened to the sobs echoing in the room, and paused a moment to let the everyone get a good look at the touching tableau.

"No further questions, Your Honor."

John and Nancy Newland looked drained, as if the battle had been lost. "Well, that's it," said John. "We're dead. It's over."

"Not yet," said Randy Keating. "I have a secret weapon."

"What?"

"Michael McCann," he said.

Everything about Michael's performance on the witness stand suggested that he was ill at ease and uncomfortable. He wore his only suit, a thick, dark wool winter-weight suit. It was scratchy and bothersome and he was sweating long before Keating put his first question.

"Mr. McCann, how much money do you make in a year?"

For a man as secretive about money as Michael, this was a particularly unpleasant question. "Uh . . . around fifteen thousand dollars a year," he mumbled.

"Could I ask you to speak up?"

"Fifteen thousand," he said. "A year."

"Not much, is it?"

"No," said Michael miserably. "But it's been enough. Mathilda's never gone without anything."

"Oh," said Keating with a smile. "I have no doubt it's been enough *so far*. How did you plan to send her to college? Or didn't you plan on it?"

Michael gripped the arms of his hard chair and tried to keep his voice steady. "There is nothing more important to me than that she be given every opportunity. There are scholarships. I can borrow. I have always been there for her, and I believe I can be there for her when that time comes."

Randy Keating did not look very convinced by these earnest, heartfelt words. "You believe? I have a belief too, Mr. McCann. I believe that if this child were the responsibility of her real father, she would be able to *without a doubt* attend the best schools. *Without a doubt* she would travel the world. *Without a doubt* she would be given the opportunities this child deserves."

Jerry Bryce jumped up. "Objection. Where's the question?"

Judge Marcus nodded. "Sustained. Get to the verb, Mr. Keating."

"Sorry, Your Honor . . ." Keating paced a few steps before asking his next question. "You feel John Newland abandoned his child, don't you?"

There was no doubt in his mind. "Yes. Absolutely."

"Sounds terrible, too, doesn't it? Sounds like a pretty heartless act—if you don't know the details. You were married once, weren't you, Mr. McCann?"

The question came from out of left field and Michael never saw it coming. He was so shocked, it took him a moment to recover his voice. "Yes."

"You left that marriage while your wife was pregnant, didn't you?"

Michael's whispered answer was almost lost in the murmur from the crowd. "But—You see, she . . ."

"Please answer the question."

"There were special circumstances. . . ."

"Yes or no, Mr. McCann."

It was April Simon who couldn't stand the

tension any longer. She leaped to her feet. "Objection!"

"Sit down," the judge ordered. "You can't object."

"Sorry," said April, slinking down in her seat.

"Mr. McCann did you abandon your pregnant wife?"

"Yes."

Keating nodded, satisfied with the answer. "Yes. In fairness, Mr. McCann, I happened to know that there were circumstances that made you guiltless when you abandoned that child, just as there are circumstances in Mr. Newland's case. Would you agree with that?"

Michael nodded. "I suppose."

"John Newland was a different person back then, just as you were different. I'm going to say some words and if you feel that they do not describe you in some ways, just stop me. Okay?"

Michael's shoulders were hunched and he could not meet Keating's steady gaze. "Yes."

"Poor." said Keating. "Unfriendly. Reclusive. Miserly. Angry. Lonely. . . ." As the attorney pronounced each word, Michael's soul sank, as if listening to the nails being hammered into his coffin.

"Lonely is probably the most damning term here. Were you lonely enough to seize a child to ease your selfish pain, lonely enough to bend the law? To collaborate in stopping the natural process of finding a suitable home for this child? I wonder how much you were in on this deception."

"Objection!" yelled Bryce. "Objection!"

"You only care what happens to yourself!"

"Objection! Judge Marcus—"

The judge held up his hand, like a cop stopping traffic. "Very well. Sustained. Mr. Keating—"

"I am finished, Your Honor."

Michael, pale and trembling, stepped down from the stand. No one doubted that he was finished as well.

"I have a headache," said Judge Marcus to his wife. He was lying flat on his back, sprawled on the sofa in his chambers. To treat the pain in his head he was sipping at a glass of scotch whiskey, neat—no ice, no water.

Mrs. Marcus frowned at her husband. "And so you should," she said sourly.

"I can't believe I have to go out there and give her to that John Newland sonovabitch."

Just beyond his office they could hear the sounds of people filing into the courtroom. The trial was over and in a moment Judge Marcus would have to mount the bench and deliver his verdict in the case of *Newland* v. *McCann*.

Mrs. Marcus snorted derisively. "Oh, that's baloney! You'd sell your mother for cat food, if you thought there was some profit in it. John Newland has owned you from the git-go."

The judge took another swig of whiskey and swung himself upright on the couch. "Well, you didn't seem to mind getting those Redskins' tickets every year. . . ."

The judge would never learn that it was unwise

to argue with his wife. "Oh, right. Like you're not dragging me out the door early so we don't miss the cheerleaders. Why don't you do something right for once?"

"I can't," the judge said wearily. "I can't go against Newland. There's too much going way back, father to father. Besides, they made their argument and it's a powerful one. It's the money, you know. How can I ask that little girl to go and live in squalor? I can't give her to McCann—not without a powerful reason." He finished his drink. "Well, better get this damn thing over with."

He looked no worse for drink when he sat down behind his tall desk. In fact, Judge Marcus looked grave and solemn and as sober as, well, a judge. There was a long silence while he shuffled his papers and looked from tense face to tense face. He hated what he was about to do, but it had to be done.

"I have come to a decision and it was a difficult one. . . . I would like to explain *why* it was so difficult." He paused for a moment, just for effect. "The happiness of a child is impossible to quantify, so I am clearly directed to look to the welfare of a child, something that can be measured in dollars and cents. Mathilda will need money for her education and for protection, for her future. . . ."

It was obvious where the decision was going. John squeezed Nancy's hand and they shared a quick, triumphant look. Michael knew as well and he felt his soul growing darker and darker, yet he was not quite able to believe that the government was going to strip him of the only thing in the world that mattered to him.

"It would be irresponsible of me to deny this child her natural claim to the wealth which is offered her."

No one noticed that at the back of the courtroom, the door swung open and Dad, the police chief, sauntered into the room. He strode down to the front of the court and hurriedly whispered something in Michael's ear. Then he crossed to John Newland and spoke to him in the same urgent manner.

". . . If it were otherwise different," Judge Marcus continued, "believe me, I would not only be obliged to go the other way, but my heart would want it to—" He stopped and glanced sharply over his spectacles. "Dad, what the hell are you doing here?"

"Approach the bench, Judge?"

The sheriff and the judge had a hurried conversation, then Marcus banged his gavel. "Change of venue!" he said. "The court will reconvene at Stone Lake!"

Most of the town assembled on the banks of the old granite quarry, standing among the building machinery and the elaborate pumping equipment that John Newland had ordered brought in to drain the lake to divert the water to his housing project.

Work had been going on for a week and the water was much reduced. With the falling water levels, the secrets of Stone Lake were being stripped away. There was no Stone Lake monster. Neither were there killer whirlpools nor clinging, strangling weeds.

However, there was a corpse.

Sprawled on the rocky bottom of the lake was a skeleton, a few tattered pieces of cloth fluttering on the bleached bones. Clutched in the skeletal fingers of the right hand was a car key, the gold Mercedes Benz three-pointed star plain to see. Scattered around the body were hundreds and hundreds of gold coins glittering in the morning sun.

"Tanny," said John Newland. His brother, with his usual sense of poor timing, had come home at last.

Only April Simon would have been capable of seeing such a ghoulish sight and the bright side at the same time. "Well, Michael, according to the morning gold quotes, it looks like you are a man of some substance . . . again."

Judge Marcus, to the immense surprise of his wife, had a sudden attack of good conscience. "As a judge," he said, "I'm always interested in the exact moment when someone's argument falls apart." He put his hand on John Newland's shoulder. "Money was *your* argument, John."

Newland was a realist and he knew when he was beaten. "I understand."

Mathilda suddenly felt sorry for the man who would have changed her life. "I'm sorry about what happened to your brother, Mr. Newland."

"Thank you," said Newland. He looked devastated, a man who had lost his brother—he had to know that he hadn't lost his daughter. "Mathilda?"

Mathilda stopped and smiled. "See you around, Mr. Newland." She walked back toward Michael.

Newland smiled weakly. It was better than nothing. . . .

Epilogue

It took a while, but Mrs. Simon did manage to track down the last resting place of Marsha Swanson. She was buried just outside of Norfolk, a sad, rundown graveyard, the final place of repose for the souls that no one cared about in life and paid no attention to now that they were gone.

Michael and Mathilda followed a custodian as he threaded a path between the unkempt graves and the thicket of decaying headstones. Mathilda carried a single white rose.

He didn't get many visitors, and like many people who work alone, he seemed anxious to talk. "Yeah," the custodian said, "we get a few folks like you every year. Lookin' for someone, everybody's looking for someone and this is the last place they look, that's for sure." He consulted an old list. "B-31. Right over there . . ."

Michael stopped, and Mathilda looked over her shoulder at him.

"Go ahead," he said, motioning her forward. "You go. This is between you and . . . you and your mom."

Mathilda walked to the low rise of grass and carefully placed the rose at the head.

She took a deep breath and began to whisper. "I found you, Mom. I wish I could see your face. . . . I guess I look a little like you."

Mathilda was silent for a moment, as if choosing her words carefully. "My name is Mathilda, but my middle name turns out to be Marsha. At the trial, Mr. Newland said he got you off drugs, but I know he didn't. *You* did it for me. . . ."

The wind blew, riffling her hair. Mathilda brushed away a tear. "I know you couldn't help what you were, and for all the things you couldn't do for me, that's okay. I understand how it must have been for you. Not easy, I guess."

Mathilda pulled a small square of blue paper from her pocket, along with a small tack. She pressed the pin through the paper, affixing the paper to the grave. Mathilda had written her name on the paper in her tiniest handwriting.

"This is just to let you know I was here," she said softly. "And don't worry about me." Mathilda looked back at Michael and smiled at him. "I'm in good hands."

SIGNET

Published or forthcoming

BEACHES

Iris Rainer Dart

Once in a lifetime you make a friendship that lasts forever ...

From the moment Cee Cee Bloom and Bertie Barron collide on the beach at Atlantic City aged ten and seven, they are friends ... for life. In time Cee Cee, a talented singer and comedienne, successfully pursues Hollywood stardom, while Bertie chooses the conventional life of marriage and motherhood. But despite the striking differences between them, the two women sustain each other through thirty years of careers and children, jealousy and drugs, lovers and divorce. And when they are torn apart by a shattering tragedy, against all odds Cee Cee and Bertie find strength in their extraordinary friendship.

'Well-written, well-constructed and thoroughly enjoyable' – *Daily Telegraph*

Published or forthcoming

A MATTER OF FAT

Sherry Ashworth

Eating is sexy, sensual, wonderful, indulgent – how could they resist temptation . . .

At the Heyside branch of Slim-Plicity the women are valiantly struggling with their waistbands while waiting for the spare flesh to melt away. Stella, their mentor, is so proud of them – they are going to be the slimmest group in the north-west, and qualify for the celebration buffet. Meanwhile, in a nearby meeting room, the unabashed members of the Fat Women's Support Group virtuously agree that dieting is a tool of women's oppression used by men and the media to torment the overweight . . .

'In *A Matter of Fat*, Ashworth has retained a wicked sense of humour, while raising some very important questions. Does she have the answers, though? You'll have to read the book if you want to find out!' – *New Woman*